This Sword for Hire

THIS SWORD FOR HIRE

by Richard Lee Byers

Rothco Press • Los Angeles, California

Published by Rothco Press
8033 West Sunset Blvd. Suite 1022
Los Angeles, CA 90046

"Troll Trouble" originally appeared in *Blackguards: Tales of Assassins, Mercenaries, and Rogues,* J. M. Martin, editor, Ragnarok Publications, 2015.
"The Salamander" originally appeared (in different form) in *Sword of Ice and Other Tales of Valedemar,* Mercedes Lackey, editor, DAW, 1997.
"Death in Keenspur House" originally appeared (in different form) in *Crossroads and Other Tales of Valdemar,* Mercedes Lackey, editor, DAW, 2005.
"The Cheat" originally appeared (in different form) in *Moving Targets and Other Tales of Valdemar,* Mercedes Lackey, editor, DAW, 2008.
"Light and Dark" originally appeared in *The Crimson Pact: Volume 2,* Paul Genesse, editor, Alliteration Ink, 2011.
"The Silent Singer" originally appeared in *The Bard's Tale: Stories and Recipes from The Black Dragon Inn,* Daniel Myers, editor, Silence in the Library, 2015.

Cover by Rob Cohen
Cover photo © Dmitrijs Bindemanis

Rothco Press is a division of Over Easy Media Inc.

First Edition

ISBN: 978-1-945436-00-0
Electronic ISBN: 978-1-945436-01-7

Also by Richard Lee Byers

Deathward

Fright Line

The Vampire's Apprentice

Dark Fortune

Dead Time

Joy Ride

Warlock Games

Party Till You Drop

The Tale of the Terrible Toys

Soul Killer

Caravan of Shadows

The Ebon Mask

Dark Kingdoms (includes The Ebon Mask and completes the story that novel began)

Netherworld

On A Darkling Plain

Forsaken

Forsworn

Forbidden

The Enemy Within

The Impostor #1: Half a Hero

The Q Word and Other Stories

The Shattered Mask

Queen of the Depths

The Black Bouquet

Dissolution

The Rage

The Rite

The Ruin

The Year of Rogue Dragons (collects The Rage, The Rite, and The Ruin plus two bonus stories)

Unclean

Undead

Unholy

The Captive Flame

Whisper of Venom

The Spectral Blaze

The Masked Witches

Prophet of the Dead

Called to Darkness

Blind God's Bluff

The Reaver

Black Dogs

The Impostor: Half a Hero

The Impostor: Blood Machine

The Ghost in the Stone

This Sword for Hire

Black Crowns (forthcoming)

The Ire of the Void (forthcoming)

The Things That Crawl (forthcoming)

Troll Trouble

The Forest of Thorns is well named. Briars scratched and snagged me with every step, or at least it seemed that way. Meanwhile, the soft ground mired my boots, and cold rainwater dripped on me from the weave of branches overhead.

In other words, this little excursion into the wild was unpleasant enough to remind me of one reason why I'd abandoned the life of a mercenary—marching in the snow and heat, eating half-spoiled rations or none at all, and sleeping rough—to set up shop as a fencing master in Balathex, City of Fountains. I strove to stay alert lest discomfort distract me.

Yet despite my caution, when I first glimpsed the troll peeking out at me, he was only a few strides away. It seemed unfair that a creature so large could nonetheless hide so successfully, even behind the broad, mossy trunk of an ancient oak.

Truly, though, there was no reason why he shouldn't, because he wasn't as tall as a tree. Such towering specimens may have existed long ago. They may still, in far corners of the world. But in all my wandering, I've never seen one.

No, his long arms knotted with muscle, hide mottled brown and gray, red eyes shining under a ridged brow and fanged mouth smirking and slavering at the prospect of cruel sport and fresh meat, this fellow merely loomed half again as tall as I was. That was still big enough to make a sensible man turn tail.

I didn't, though. Nor did I reach for my broadsword in its scabbard, though my fingers itched for the hilt. Instead, as the creature shambled into the open, I gave him a nod and said, "Hello. My name is Selden. I come as an envoy of the August Assembly of Balathex."

Then I studied his brutish face in an effort to determine whether he believed the lie, and if so, whether it mattered.

*

My errand began three nights earlier, in the shop I'd rented and through hard and fumbling work—I'm no carpenter—transformed into a space suitable for teaching swordplay and associated arts. Effort wasted, it seemed, for no students had presented themselves to study there.

The problem was that I was a stranger. No one in Balathex knew me as a successful duelist or an instructor capable of raising others to proficiency. The obvious remedy was to pick a few quarrels, but I was reluctant to go down that path.

I'd grown tired of killing for no better reason than to put silver in my purse, and besides, I was loath to start my new life by instigating feuds. I didn't need vengeful brothers, sons, and friends of the deceased leaping out at me for years thereafter.

Unfortunately, that unsatisfactory scheme was the only plan I'd been able to devise. Thus, on the night in question, I sat alone drinking cheap Ghentoy red laced with raw spirit, and never mind that I'd squandered coin originally intended for next week's rent to purchase the jugs. Morose as I was, I had more immediate needs.

Someone rapped on the door.

My first half-tipsy thought was that I'd lost track of the date, and the landlord had come for his due, but a moment's reflection assured me that couldn't be so. Perhaps here was my first pupil, then, unlikely as that seemed at this late hour.

I straightened my jerkin, smoothed down my hair, and hurried to answer the knock. When I did, a stooped old woman squinted at me from the other side of the door.

She wore charms, talismans of made of bone and feathers and other items hidden in little cloth bags, dangling around her wrinkled neck. But had you seen her, you wouldn't have thought sorceress. You would have thought witch.

For there was nothing about her to suggest the sort of citified mage who pores over grimoires, compounds elixirs from rare ingredients, and commands devils via complex ritual and force of will. Rather, she was manifestly a village wise woman who knew only the patchy lore her mother passed down to her, brewed dubious remedies from whatever happened to grow nearby, and dickered with goblins in a manner little different than she'd haggle with a neighbor.

Surprised, I said, "Mother Elkinda."

She sniffed twice. "You stink of drink."

"Whereas you stink of the usual." It was true. There are rustic folk who give the lie to the insult dirty peasant, but she wasn't one of them. "And I suppose that as we both smell already, a hug won't make it any worse."

We put that to the test, and afterward, I ushered her inside.

"How did you know I was in the city?" I asked.

"The wind whispered it to me, and then I dowsed my way to your door." She hefted a gnarled walking stick.

"Well, it's good you came when you did," I said. "In a week or two, I'll likely be gone." Soldiering again, if I could find a captain to take me on this late in the season.

I don't think she even registered the glumness in my tone. "I need your help," she said. "I…may have done a bad thing."

Concern nudged aside my self-pity. I waved her on toward the rickety table.

She stumbled before she got there. It was a long hike from her little forest village to the city, and she'd exhausted herself making it. I caught her, got her into a chair, poured her a cup of wine, and sat back down across from her. "Tell me," I said.

She took a long drink first. When she set the goblet down, she said, "There are trolls in the wood."

More concerned now, I nodded. "I know."

"Well, what you may not know is that sometimes they need blessings and medicine just like people do. Then they come to me."

I frowned. "That's like trafficking with outlaws, only worse. People would hang you if they found out."

She glowered. "I give the trolls things they need, and in return, they leave the village alone. We couldn't live where we do, otherwise."

"I can believe it," I said. "And I wasn't condemning you, just worried for your sake. Please, go on."

"Well...two of the trolls who came to me were Skav Hearteater, their chieftain, and Ojojum, his mate. Their problem was, she couldn't conceive."

"And that upset them?"

"Yes. In some ways, trolls and people are alike. Through my craft, I discovered the fault lay with Skav, but when I tried to quicken his seed with the usual remedies, nothing happened."

"So you tried something unusual?"

"Once I was fool enough to tell the trolls the notion that had come to me, they insisted. Had I refused, how do you think it would have ended?"

"With your flesh in their bellies," I said. "So what did you do?"

"I called a spirit of lust and fertility and put it inside the Hearteater. My thought was that he would share the imp's vigor the next time he and Ojojum coupled." She smiled. "And I was right. She's with child."

"Then what's the problem?"

The smile disappeared. "Skav changed. He'd always doted on Ojojum. But afterward, he started beating her until, fearful she'd lose the baby, she ran away."

"Ran away and came to you. Because she suspected your magic was to blame? More to the point, do you think it's to blame?"

Elkinda sighed. "Perhaps. When the spirit came, I sensed it was something crueler and less biddable than I meant to catch. Something from the netherworld and not just out of Nature."

"You should have tossed it back and tried again."

"That's easy to say now, but I'd had trouble summoning anything. I didn't know if I'd be lucky a second time, and with the trolls watching and waiting…"

"I understand," I said. "Well, partly. Do you believe the spirit's touch poisoned Skav's mind?"

"Worse. I fear it didn't leave his body when it was supposed to. I need you to find out if it's still inside."

"What, now?"

"I can fix it so you're able to see the incubus once you're close enough. I need to know for a fact that it's there and how it looks before I can set about casting it out."

"Then go peer at Skav yourself. You're the one who's friendly with him."

She shook her head. "The spirit would be suspicious of me."

"Whereas the trolls will eat me simply because they're hungry."

She grimaced. "I know what I'm asking. But dangerous as trolls are, the ones hereabout mostly leave people alone. They won't do that much longer if a demon has possessed their chief. They'll start hunting humans every chance they get, and you're the only one I can ask to help me keep it from happening."

She didn't add that I owed her my life. Apparently she trusted me to remember that for myself.

I came down with the plague called the Bloody Noose when my mercenary company was chasing bandits on the fringe of the Forest of Thorns. For fear of contagion, my comrades abandoned me. Mother Elkinda found me a day later.

She always claimed the foul potions and gruels she gave me cured me of my affliction. I had my doubts. But I didn't doubt that after the delirium passed and I was breathing normally again, my lingering weakness would still have killed me had she not nursed me through the two long months of my recovery.

Now the debt had come due. I poured us each another drink and said, "Tell me how I'll be able to spot the imp."

*

Now you know how I came to find myself deep in the woods facing a troll. But you may still wonder why I approached the creatures openly when I might have spied on them instead.

This was my thinking. Mother Elkinda knew the trolls watched the trails in the heart of the wood but not where they laired. I could have crept around for days before I found the place, and even when I had, I might not recognize Skav. I'd never seen him before, and to human eyes, one naked beast-man tends to looks like another. And once I did identify him, I'd still need to come close to discern the incubus inside, close enough to make concealment problematic.

Thus, passing myself off as an emissary seemed a better option. Or at least it did until the troll roared and rushed me with ham-sized, jagged-clawed hands outstretched.

I jumped aside, and he lunged past me. As he lurched back around, I snatched my sword out. He hesitated, but not, I judged, because the blade frightened him. He was simply considering how to contend with it.

At least that gave me another chance to talk. "I know where Ojojum is," I told him. "I think the Hearteater will want to hear, don't you?"

"Yes," he growled, then instantly swatted at the sword in an attempt to knock it aside.

I twitched the blade above the arc of the blow and sliced him across the knuckles. He snatched his hand back, and in that instant, I lunged closer and set sharp steel against his dangling, warty genitals. He froze.

"Give me your word," I said, "that you'll take me to Skav without any more nonsense. Or I swear I'll geld you."

"I'll take you," he said. His voice still sounded like growls and coughs. It reminded me of the lions I'd seen in the grasslands of Lazvalla.

I shifted my sword away from his maleness and returned it to its scabbard. I didn't like doing it, but it seemed unwieldy to approach Skav as an envoy and a hostage taker, too.

To my relief, the creature before me didn't try another attack. Instead, he led me on down the path. Evidently the feel of a blade against his tender parts had made a lasting impression.

His cooperation notwithstanding, I never dropped my guard. But eventually I relaxed somewhat, and then I asked, "What sort of mood is the Hearteater in today?"

My guide gave me a glower. "Angry. Hungry." Then he stepped into a spot where the tangle of branches overhead was thin and winced at the wan light leaking down from the sky.

That's how trolls are. It's a myth that sunlight turns them to stone, but they're sensitive to it. Had my companion not been charged with keeping watch on the trail, he might well have opted to sleep by day and roam around at night.

Certainly, that was the case with the majority of his fellows. They lay snoring in heaps of leaves and pine needles in a particularly shady portion of the forest floor.

Despite the crudity of the sleeping arrangements, the place had the air of a home and not just a camp where nomads had stopped for a day. The trolls had taken the trouble to wedge racks of antlers and skulls, some of them human, in the crotches of trees and to scratch crude drawings on the trunks.

That was all I had time to take in before one of the wakeful trolls noticed me. He roared a warning, whereupon his fellows roused and, glaring and slavering, came shambling to surround me.

I didn't realize when one reached to grab me from behind. Fortunately, my guide noticed. He snarled, slashed with his claws, and sent my would-be assailant reeling backward with a gashed face.

It was more assistance than I had any right to expect. But I'd entered the trolls' home at the side of my reluctant escort, and maybe that meant an attempt to harm me implied disrespect for him.

The balked troll swiped at his flowing blood and gathered himself to lunge. Fearing that a general brawl was imminent, I shouted, "I speak for the lords of Balathex, and I can tell you what's become of Ojojum!"

Some part of that was surprising or intriguing enough to make the creatures around me falter. Then another troll, one who hadn't rushed to encircle me with the others, prowled out of the gloom.

Upon observing him, I decided I'd been wrong about one thing. I would have recognized Skav Hearteater on sight. He was even bigger than the others and had dried blood and yellow earth streaked on his face and chest.

I couldn't tell if he also had an incubus riding him. I hoped Elkinda's witchcraft would answer that question in due course.

"What do you know about my mate?" Skav demanded.

"One thing at a time," I said. "Do you understand that I speak for Balathex?"

He flicked his hand in an impatient gesture I chose to interpret as yes.

"So do you promise to receive me hospitably and allow me to depart in peace," I persisted, "as the rulers of men deal with one another's envoys?"

"Tell me where Ojojum is!" he bellowed, "or my people will tear you to bits!" The trolls surrounding me poised their hands to rip and snatch.

"Kill me," I said, "and you won't find out about your mate. More, if I don't come home in one piece, Balathex will avenge the affront to its sovereignty by sending an army to scour the forest clean of trolls, as many of my folk believe we should have long ago."

Skav glared at me. I stared back while trying to look like a dauntless idiot who'd enjoy nothing more than dying hideously for the sake of the Whispering City.

Finally the Hearteater said, "I promise not to hurt you. Why not? What does a little turd like you matter either way?"

"Thank you for your courtesy," I replied. "May I approach?"

"Come," he said, and, looking disgruntled that I might not be supper after all, the other trolls opened the way for me. I walked forward until I was near enough to converse comfortably, which in this circumstance wasn't comfortable at all.

Without taking my eyes off Skav, I bowed. "My lord—"

"Ojojum!" he snapped. "Where?"

"Balathex," I replied.

"You captured her." His clawed fingers flexed, and growls and muttering sounded from the trolls behind me.

"No," I said. "She came to the city of her own free will seeking sanctuary, and the August Assembly gave it to her."

He hesitated. Then: "You're lying!"

I certainly was. Had his mate presented herself at a city gate, the guard would have attacked her on sight. But I hoped ignorance of human society would prevent Skav from realizing how preposterous my claims actually were.

"Admittedly," I said, "it's a novel situation. But your mate's petition came to the attention of the Handmaids of Rendeth. The welfare of mothers and children is their particular concern, and they pleaded on Ojojum's behalf."

"For a troll! And the leaders heeded them!"

"Yes. They respect the temples, and honestly, I think the very strangeness of it all intrigued them." Trying to look casual about it, I drew a handkerchief from my sleeve, ostensibly to wipe sweat from my face. In reality, Mother Elkinda had soaked the cloth in something she'd brewed in an iron pot, and I needed to get the fumes into my eyes.

When I did, my eyes burned, and tears dissolved the world into blur. I daresay blindness is never desirable, but I can attest that unexpectedly losing your sight in the midst of a mob of man-eating brutes is particularly disconcerting.

Fortunately, none of the trolls availed itself of the opportunity to attack me before the stinging faded and I blinked and wiped the tears away. Instead, Skav asked me, "What ails you?"

"Pardon me," I said. Meanwhile, inside my head, I was cursing Elkinda for not warning me. "Apparently something's blooming hereabouts…"

Suddenly, midway through my excuse, Skav's face changed. A second set of features shined through it like firelight glowing through a paper lantern, and remarkably, the one underneath was even more disturbing. With his crooked fangs and piggy crimson eyes, the troll chieftain was ugly and intimidating but not unnatural. In contrast, the long, narrow visage of the incubus twitched, oozed, and flickered from moment to moment in a way that was both wrong in some fundamental manner and sickening to behold.

But I couldn't let the demon know I beheld it. I held myself steady and finished my thought: "…that disagrees with me."

"I'll disagree with you," said Skav, jumping back to the actual point of the conversation, "unless you prove you're telling the truth."

"Just think about it," I replied. "If Ojojum didn't come to Balathex, how do I even know her name, let alone that she's gone missing?"

Apparently he couldn't think of an alternative explanation. For after another pause, he snarled, "Send her back! Or I'll kill every human in the forest!"

Now that I had the information I'd come for, I would have liked nothing better than to assure him Balathex would bow to his wishes and make a speedy departure. But alas, the emissary I was pretending to be wouldn't behave that way.

"We've been over this," I said. "If you trolls make pests of yourselves, the August Assembly will do whatever is required to exterminate you. But it needn't come to that. Ojojum wants to return home."

Skav grunted. "What's stopping her, then?"

"You are. She says you've been beating her for no reason, and she's afraid she'll miscarry."

He hesitated. Then: "There are reasons. But maybe I've been too strict. I don't want to hurt the child." Behind its mask of flesh, the incubus grinned.

"Good," I said. "But it won't be quite that easy. When Ojojum returns, six Handmaids will accompany her. They'll ask you to swear on a lock of Rendeth's hair that the abuse will stop."

The incubus's leer stretched until it split his seething face in two. "If that's what it takes."

After negotiating the details of the fictitious rendezvous, I took my leave and quickened my pace once I was a little way down the trail. Shortly after that, I had to stop and puke. The devil's face had been that upsetting.

*

When I told Mother Elkinda about the palaver, she said, "You didn't tell me you were going to talk to them. It's a wonder you're still alive."

I shrugged. "I made Skav believe he had to let me go to seize a bigger prize, namely, Ojojum at his mercy once more, six nuns to eat, and a sacred relic to defile. What I don't understand is why he and the tribe aren't rampaging through the woods killing people already."

The witch shifted on the only chair in her hut. "Maybe the incubus wants to get used to being Skav first," she said. "Or spend more time enjoying it. The spirit may believe that once the slaughter starts, an army truly will come running to wipe out the trolls, its host included."

"Too bad that isn't so."

When the residents of Balathex thought about the forest dwellers at all, it was as poachers, runaway indentured servants, and mad hermits whose welfare was of trifling importance. In time, I supposed, the August Assembly might send sufficient troops to put an end to the trolls, but by then, whole settlements would lie dead.

"No use crying about it." Throwing her head back, Elkinda emptied her jack of the bitter beer they brewed there in her village, then used her walking stick to heave herself to her feet. "I'll just have to clean up my own mess." She started hobbling around gathering the ingredients for a spell, a clump of moss from this shelf, a piece of stag horn carved with a rune from the table in the corner.

I stood up from the earthen floor so I could stay out of her way. My head jostled a dried lizard hanging beneath the thatched roof.

When Elkinda had collected everything she needed, she carried it outside to the crackling yellow fire she'd built, and I followed. She gazed up at the moon and stars, or what we could see of them through crisscrossing branches and wisps of cloud, then motioned for me to stand in a particular spot.

I couldn't tell what made that bit of ground special. She hadn't scratched a circle of protection in the dirt or anything like that. But I obeyed without asking the reason why. Once mages set to work, it's dangerous to distract them.

With me positioned to her satisfaction, the wise woman started chanting words in a language I didn't recognize. Periodically, she tossed one of the items she'd collected into the flames until they were all gone. Afterward, the incantation droned on.

Then, in an instant, the fire turned from gold to scarlet and shot up high over Elkinda's head. At the top, the pillar of flame spread into a fan shape in a way that reminded me of a hand poised to swat a fly.

Elkinda gasped and jerked backward. She recognized the threat as quickly as I did, but that didn't mean she was spry enough to avoid it.

I lunged, threw my arms around her, and drove onward until balance deserted me and we fell. Behind us, fire hurtled earthward with a hiss like a cataract. A wave of heat washed over me.

But when I checked, neither Elkinda nor I were burning, nor had the plunging blaze left a sheet of flame licking at our feet. Some tufts of grass were charring and smoking, but mostly, the fire was gone. In the pit where the witch had lit it with a word of command, only coals remained.

I stood up, offered my hand, and hauled her to her feet. "Are you all right?" I asked.

"No," she said.

"Did I hurt you? I didn't want to knock you down—"

"I'm fine!" she spat. "But don't you understand what just happened? I can't cast out the incubus! It's protected. Too much darkness stuck to it when I pulled it up from the places underneath."

"Maybe if you try again?"

"I will. I owe everyone that, no matter what the danger. But it won't work."

"Then don't be foolish. Think of a different tactic."

She shook her head. "There's only one. I'd need to attack the incubus close up, with Skav in front of my eyes. That might tip the balance in my favor. But how could I do it without the trolls spotting me?"

How indeed?

Curse it, it wasn't fair. I'd called on the trolls once and lived to tell about it. That should have been sufficient.

But there isn't much in life that counts for less than fair and should. I took a breath and said, "Well, plainly, you can't creep up on them, not tottering along with a cane. We'll need to hide you where the creatures will come to you. And then I'll need to distract them."

*

My second meeting with the trolls was set for dusk. Plainly, that was stupid. Even if a man survived the parley itself, he'd start the night in the deep forest for the man-eaters to stalk as the temptation seized them. But when Skav and I negotiated the details of the rendezvous, I hadn't imagined I'd actually be keeping it.

As Ojojum and I advanced up the trail, I resisted the urge to look for other trolls. It didn't matter if they were already shadowing us. The important question was, had the creatures stumbled across Mother Elkinda in the thicket where I'd hidden her that morning?

Unfortunately, there was no way of knowing, and perhaps Ojojum realized as much, for she, with her tangled steel-gray tresses and unborn child swelling her belly, looked as nervous as I felt. After a while, I noticed she was shivering.

It sounds asinine to say I felt sympathy for a troll, but perhaps it was because we were comrades in a dangerous venture. I touched her on the forearm, above the spot where some animal's teeth or horns had scarred her, and said, "It's going to be all right."

She shook her head. "I didn't tell Mother Elkinda everything Skav did to me. Beatings weren't the worst of it."

"It wasn't truly him," I said. "That's why we're here, to bring the real Skav back."

"I know." She spat in the dirt as a soldier will try to spit away fear. I shifted my hold on the chest tucked under my arm, and we headed onward.

I'd carried the box around through years of campaigning, and though I'd done my best to clean it up, it still looked like the scratched, utilitarian article it was. But I hoped that to troll eyes, it would pass for a reliquary.

After another bend, the trail widened out to make a clearing. Concealed by brush, a stream gurgled nearby.

Skav was waiting with much of his tribe but not, I was relieved to see, with a killed or captured Elkinda. Upon sighting Ojojum and me, he asked, "Where are the Handmaids of Rendeth?"

"I apologize," I said. "When the time to set forth arrived, it turned out that even holy sisters are susceptible to human frailty.

By which I mean, they were afraid to meet trolls. But surely that doesn't matter. You see Ojojum is with me. I also brought the relic." I held out the chest.

Meanwhile, I prayed my nattering had fixed everyone's attention on me. That Elkinda had lit her fire—she'd said she could manage with a small one, but the exorcism required at least a bit of flame—and started whispering her incantation without anyone noticing.

Skav glowered as though pondering whether there might be some way of forcing me to produce the absent nuns. Finally his red eyes shifted to Ojojum. "Have you truly come back to me?" he asked.

She hesitated, and the thought came to me that our deception was about to fail because she was too afraid to lie convincingly. But then she said, "You hurt me and shamed me, but a child needs a father. I'll come back if you take the oath."

"Good." The Hearteater looked back to me. "Open the box."

"As you wish." I set the chest on the ground slowly, feigning reverence. Then I slipped the iron key into the lock and tried to twist it.

It wouldn't turn. Since I'd previously broken the lock with the point of a dagger, that didn't surprise me.

But I did my best to feign surprise. As I jiggled and shifted the key, I said, "I'm sorry. I didn't try this before I left the temple. The Handmaids didn't warn me the lock sticks."

Skav endured my clicking the key back and forth for a bit longer. Then a clawed hand gripped my shoulder and flung me backward. The troll chieftain dropped to one knee beside the chest and started trying to turn the key himself.

Why, you may wonder, did he bother? He surely intended to end this farce by giving Ojojum the most vicious thrashing yet and telling his fellow trolls to tear me apart. Why not get on with it, then?

I can only speculate, but maybe the incubus simply wasn't very clever. With the right bit of mummery, you could fix its attention on something insignificant.

Or maybe it enjoyed toying with its victims and so didn't care to reveal its true intentions just yet. It wanted Ojojum and me to enjoy false hope a while longer.

While Skav fiddled with the key, I silently implored Elkinda to hurry and fought the urge to glance in her direction. I wanted to know if there were at least wisps of smoke rising from the thicket, but I couldn't risk some troll looking where I was and spotting them, too.

Skav eventually snarled, sprang to his feet, and grabbed the chest. His claws digging into the wood, making it snap and groan, he swung it over his head.

"Please, don't!" I cried. "The chest is sacred in its own right!"

Ignoring me, he dashed the box to the ground. It smashed apart to reveal the emptiness inside.

The Hearteater rounded on me. "What does this mean?" he growled.

It meant I needed to improvise a new stalling tactic.

"It's a miracle," I said. "Rendeth whisked the lock of hair out of the chest and back to the temple."

Ridiculous as that assertion sounded, it gave Skav pause. His true plans for the relic had surely been impious to say the least, and perhaps in his mind, that bad intent lent my claim a trace of plausibility.

As before, his hesitation didn't last long. Then he said, "The hair was never in there."

"It was," I insisted. "I saw it myself before the Handmaids closed the chest. And I know what this means." I turned to Ojojum. "You said you had to return to Skav for the baby's sake and so we could never be together. But the Bright Angel has given us a sign that our love is meant to be."

The trolls gaped at me. The notion of romance between one of their kind and a human was as bizarre to them as it is to you and me.

But grotesquerie was helpful. Anything to keep Skav off balance.

Ojojum was as surprised as everyone else and needed a moment to reply. When she did, though, she followed my lead: "Yes. You're kind, and Skav's cruel. You're clever, and he's stupid. You'll make a better mate and a better father."

Seemingly furious and dumbfounded in equal measure, Skav looked like he was struggling to work out a suitable response. Eventually he opted for the obvious.

"Enough of this craziness!" he roared to his followers. "Come eat." He sneered at Ojojum. "You're going to eat his face, eyes, and pizzle, and afterward, I'll fix it so you never run off again."

Some of the trolls, the hungrier or less befuddled ones, started toward me. I drew my broadsword. The blade glowed white in the gathering gloom.

"Another miracle!" I cried. "Rendeth charged the sword with holy power."

I wished. The humbler truth was that Elkinda, loath to send me back among the trolls without some semblance of a magical defense, had muttered over the weapon and then set it outside for the better part of a day, during which time it had soaked up sunlight like a sponge holds water.

The trolls balked. The radiance stung and dazzled them, and maybe they feared the Bright Angel truly was watching over me.

But then Skav decided she wasn't. Or else the infernal spirit inhabiting him was game to try its luck against an agent of the divine.

The troll chieftain advanced on me. I came on guard, my sword held high to shine as much light in his eyes as possible.

This was pretty much the situation all my trickery and lies were supposed to avert. The sole difference between it and my grimmest imaginings was that I was only fighting Skav. For the moment, his followers were holding back, but it was far from certain that would change the outcome in my favor, especially when I couldn't even try for the kill. I still hoped that, given enough time, Elkinda would cast the demon out.

Squinting against the glow, Skav came closer still, then, with a quicker, lunging step, snatched for the broadsword. Though I didn't want to kill him, I was willing to wound him if that would slow him down, and I spun the blade to avoid the grab and slice his hand as I'd previously cut the watcher on the trail.

Skav spun his hand, too, and swept the sword out of line. He sprang and raked at my chest with his claws. The other trolls roared in anticipation of the killing stroke.

I leaped backward, and the attack fell short by a finger-length. He kept charging and slashing, and I continued my scrambling retreat. I tried to open up the distance so I could interpose my blade between us again, but he was pressing too hard.

Then I attempted a shift to the side that would cause him to blunder past me. He compensated.

In desperation, I suddenly reversed direction, advancing instead of retreating. That spoiled his aim, and his talons slashed harmlessly behind me. I bashed the broadsword's pommel into his jaw. If the impact stunned him, it would win me the instant I needed to separate myself from him and come back on guard. If not, I'd positioned myself perfectly for him to gather me into a flensing, bone-breaking bear hug.

The attack did stun him. Even so, simply by stumbling on forward, he nearly knocked me to the ground. But I wrenched myself out of the way and even managed to cut the back of his thigh as I did.

Unfortunately, though, when Skav shook off the daze produced by the clout on the jaw and whirled in my direction, he moved as fast as before. The leg wound didn't hinder him.

The thing that was hampering him was the sunlight stored in the sword. That became apparent when it dimmed and disappeared.

The trolls bellowed and howled to see the enchantment exhaust its power, and Skav came at me even harder. He could now see me better.

Whereas I was seeing him worse. With the glow in the blade extinguished, I discovered that if the sun hadn't quite set yet, it might as well have with the trees obscuring it.

Curse you, Elkinda, I thought, and curse my stupidity, too. Why had I staked my life on a second exorcism succeeding when the first one had been an abject failure?

I belatedly decided I should try to kill the Hearteater. If I succeeded, the trolls wouldn't have a demon for a leader anymore and presumably wouldn't go on a rampage. That would be victory of a sort even if I doubted the creatures would let me survive to celebrate it.

Since I'd been fighting defensively, when I came on the attack, it surprised Skav. A stop cut met a clawing hand and left the little finger dangling. He hesitated. I stepped in, feinted high, then low, then spun my blade high again to deliver the true attack at the juncture of his neck and shoulder. The cut landed where I'd aimed it.

But Skav drove at me once more. Leathery hide and dense muscle had kept the sword stroke from shearing deep enough to kill.

I jumped back. His claws still grazed my chest, though, and that was enough to dump me on the ground.

Skav threw himself on top of me. The hand I'd maimed retained sufficient strength to pin my sword arm. The Hearteater raised the intact one to rip me to pieces.

Then Ojojum rushed in behind him, grabbed his wrist, and strained to keep him from clawing me. Her intervention roused the rest of the trolls from their passivity, and they charged forward, too. I had no doubt it was to pull her off Skav and enable him to get on with butchering me.

But that was when the incubus finally came swirling up out of the troll chieftain's head like steam from a kettle.

The spirit's long, rippling face seemed even ghastlier than before, because now it was full of rage and the rage was directed at me. Its cloudy arms stretching, it reached down and plunged its fingers into my head.

Its touch felt like what it was, filth slithering into me, but there was even more to the unpleasantness than that. Every nasty thing in my mind—emotions it had shamed me to feel, perverse impulses I didn't even realize I had—welled up to join with the intruder.

Given time, that dual onslaught would surely have crushed my will. But when Elkinda dragged the spirit out of him, Skav had gone limp. His grip on my sword arm had relaxed, and I was able to jerk it free.

I thrust the blade through the demon's torso and felt nothing. It was like stabbing fog.

Still, perhaps because Elkinda's magic rendered it susceptible, the incubus screeched, a shriek heard not with the ears but with the mind, and disappeared. To my relief, the vile sensations in my head vanished along with it.

Afterward, the trolls stood flummoxed by astonishment and conceivably even horror. For it seemed to me that the incubus's appearance had appalled them, too.

In that moment of quiet, Elkinda emerged from her thicket. "There," she declared, "all better."

Still heedless of his various wounds, Skav got up off me and embraced Ojojum. "I couldn't help it," he growled. "The spirit had me in its grip."

"I know." She ran her talons through his greasy black hair, dislodging a nit or two. "I know."

Skav rounded on Elkinda. "I should have said," he growled, "the spirit had me in its grip thanks to you."

I clambered to my feet. "You're right," I panted. "The wise woman's magic didn't work precisely as intended. But she and I risked our lives to save you, and at the end of it all, you and Ojojum have the child you wanted. That being so, I ask you to let Elkinda and me go in peace."

Scowling, the troll mulled it over. Then he asked, "All the things you said before. About being an envoy, the relic, and loving Ojojum. Was any of it true?"

"Not a bit," I said.

He laughed a grating laugh. "The demon believed, but I didn't. All right. Go."

I took a long breath and strode toward Elkinda.

Then Skav said, "Wait."

Heart thumping, I turned.

"We have gold," said the troll. "Some, our fathers took fighting yours. Some, we take from city fools who hunt too deep inside the forest. Do you want any?"

I did. I knew just what to do with it.

With gold, I could rent a more fashionable space for my school, buy elegant clothes, and cut a stylish figure to attract the notice of Balathex's gentry. I could stage fencing exhibitions and demonstrate my skills. Gold was a second chance to achieve the life I wanted.

I smiled at Skav. "Well, if you're offering," I said.

The Salamander

By my reckoning, the arsonist might strike in any of fifteen places. It was sheer luck, if that's the right term, that I'd chosen to guard the right location.

When it happened, it happened fast. One moment, I was prowling the cramped recesses of the tiring house of the Azure Swan Theater. Painted actors frantically changing costume squirmed past me glaring at the intruder blocking the way. Their ill will didn't bother me half as much as the flowery rhetoric being declaimed on stage. That night's play was The Bride and the Battle-axe, a tragedy that blends mawkish sentimentality with a flawless ignorance of life on the Isle of Lentilec. Suffering through a particularly lachrymose soliloquy, I wished that the theater would catch fire, just to terminate the performance.

Try not to think things like that. One never knows what gods are listening.

An instant later, I heard a boom. Some of the audience cried out, and the forty year-old ingénue ranting on stage faltered in mid-lament. Something began to hiss and crackle. I scrambled to the nearest of the rear-stage entrances, looked out, and saw that a patch of thatch on the roof of the left-hand gallery was burning.

Then the straw above the royal family's empty box exploded into flame. The two fires raced along the roof like lovers rushing to embrace. At the same time, they oozed down the columns into the topmost of the three tiers of seats. I peered about, but could see no sign of the enemy I'd been hired to stop.

Shrieking people shoved along the galleries toward the stairs. Others climbed over the railings and dropped into the cobbled courtyard, where they joined the stampede of groundlings driving toward the exit at the rear of the enclosure. In half a minute, the passage was jammed.

It was plain that not everyone would make it out that way. There was a stage door in the back of the tiring house, but none of the audience had come in that way, nor was it visible from any of their vantage points, so none of them thought to use it.

Abandoning my efforts to spot the incendiary, I ran forward past two wooden columns painted to resemble marble to the foot of the stage. Though the blaze had yet to descend past the highest gallery, I could already feel the heat. "This way!" I shouted. "There's another exit!"

Nobody paid the least attention. Perhaps, between the roar of the fire and the panicky cries, no one heard.

I jumped off the platform, grabbed a strapping, towheaded youth with bloodstained sleeves—a butcher's apprentice, I imagine—and tried to turn him around. "Come with me!" I said.

He snarled and threw a roundhouse punch at my head. I ducked and hit him in the belly. He doubled over. I manhandled him toward the stage. "I'm trying to help you," I said. "There's another way out. Go behind the stage. The door will be on your right. Do you understand?" Evidently he did, because when I let him go, he clambered onto the proscenium.

I induced several other people to head backstage. Eventually, others noticed them going, and followed.

Which soon threatened to create a second crush, at the rear-stage doors. I sprang onto the platform and dashed back there to manage the flow of traffic as best I could, with pleas when possible and my hands when necessary.

By now the air was gray with smoke. I kept coughing. The Heavens—the machine room above me, the underside of which was painted to resemble the sky—started burning. Sparks and scraps of flaming debris rained down.

At last the stage was clear. My handkerchief pressed to my face, I scurried toward the exit. The ceiling burst.

A windlass, used to lower the actors portraying gods and their regalia, plummeted through the breach and struck where I'd just been standing. The impact shattered the floorboards.

When I escaped the playhouse, I trotted some distance away, not only to make sure that I was out of danger but to better survey the overall situation. Turning, I noticed something strange.

Fortunately, the Azure Swan stood on a spit of land that stuck out into the river. It wasn't close to any other structure. For a while, the flames enveloping the building swayed this way and that, as if groping for some other edifice they could spread to. At times they appeared to move against the breeze.

*

Sometime later, those of us who had sought to defend the theater regrouped in a private room in a nearby tavern. This council of war included several blades of the Snow Lynx political faction, which vied with the Gray Steels, Crimson Orchids, Sons of the Comet, and most bitterly with the Green Peregrines for control of Balathex, an equal number of their retainers, Draydech the sorcerer, and myself. And a singed, grimy, malodorous, and surly lot we were, too. Also present was Lady Elthea, widow of a middling prominent Snow Lynx leader, owner of the three businesses that had thus far burned, and my employer. Though elderly and infirm, she'd insisted on venturing forth from her mansion to view the site of the latest disaster.

"All right," I said, "we searched the Swan beforehand, without finding any incendiary devices. Did anyone see a figure on the roof? Or any flaming missiles?" The other men shook their heads. "Then it's magic kindling these fires, Lady Elthea. That's the only logical explanation." I looked at Draydech. "Do you concur?"

The warlock was a short fellow in his late thirties, younger than I, though with his wobbling paunch, graying goatee, and the broken veins in his bulbous nose, he looked older. He'd served his apprenticeship living rough with the nomadic Walking Oak wizards of the deep forests. Afterwards, he'd embraced the amenities of civilization with a vengeance. I'd never seen him eat a raw piece of fruit or vegetable, drink water, or go out in inclement weather. Nevertheless, he'd lost none of the skills he'd mastered in the wilderness. He was particularly adept at sniffing out mystical energies, and despite his exorbitant fees and extortionate habits, I retained him whenever that kind of witchy bloodhound work seemed likely to be in order.

Now, however, raising his eyes from the chunk of amber he'd been staring into while the rest of us glumly guzzled our wine, he said, "Certainly it's magic. Judging from the appearance of the conflagration, someone's conjured a salamander, a being from the Elemental Plane of Fire, to do the job. But I can't find it."

I scowled. "Old friend. This is not the time to angle for more gold."

Lady Elthea extended her trembling hand. Her skin was like parchment, her knuckles, swollen with arthritis. "Sorcerer, I beseech you. Some of our fellow citizens died tonight. More could perish tomorrow. If you can help prevent this, don't hold back."

Jarnac, one of the Snow Lynx blades, rose from the trestle table. "I'll take care of it, Lady Elthea," he said. He was a lanky, sandy-haired youth, dressed lavishly but not tastefully in a sapphire-and-ruby-studded parti-colored doublet with intricately carved ivory buttons. At his side hung the latest rage, one of the new smallswords, this one sporting a golden hilt. Smallswords looked elegant, and were adequate for fighting another gentleman similarly equipped. But they were apt to prove too flimsy against a heavier weapon or an armored foe, which was why I was still lugging my broadsword around.

As might have been inferred from Jarnac's ostentation, he was New Money, with a parvenu's eagerness to parade his wealth and sense of style; unlike most of his cronies in the room, he couldn't claim kinship with one of the Ancient Kindreds. Not that that mattered to me. My birth was considerably humbler than his.

He dropped a fat purse on the table. Coin clinked. "Take it, magician," he urged. "And rest assured, there's plenty more where that came from."

Draydech gazed longingly at the money. I fancy he came close to licking his lips. But at last he shook his head and said, "I can't take it, sir, because I'm not sure I can earn it. Despite Master Selden's slander"—he shot me a reproachful glance, which, given our shared history, failed to inspire any remorse—"I wasn't trying to inflate my price. Rather, I was attempting to explain that something odd has happened.

"We all should have seen the salamander. They're not invisible, quite the contrary. Even if its summoner veiled it in a glamour, I should still have spotted it. But I didn't.

"What's more, I've been sitting here scrying, and I can't pick up its trail. Apparently someone's developed a cunning new type of cloaking spell."

Sensing that he was telling the truth, I said, "And until you work out how to pierce the charm, you can't banish the spook, or guide us to its master either. Is that about the gist of it?"

"I'm afraid so."

I sighed. "What more can you tell us about salamanders?"

"A sorcerer enlists the aid of an elemental by opening a gate to its home plane, than bartering for its services. It was probably fairly easy to recruit a salamander to start fires. They love to do it anyway. The trick will be to make sure it only burns what the summoner wants it to."

Fire is a deadly threat to any town and, remembering how the theater blaze had flowed against the wind, the beginnings of a headache tightening my brow, I wondered how our problem could get any worse. The answer was immediately forthcoming.

Pivor, Lady Elthea's grandnephew and closest living kin, sprang up from his bench. He did belong to an Ancient Kindred, and no mistaking it. He had the kind of exquisite features and supercilious carriage that only generations of controlled inbreeding can produce. "Enough of this prattle," he said. "The mage has already admitted he can't aid us, so we'll have to help ourselves. We know who to blame for our troubles: the Green Peregrines." The company murmured agreement. They'd all seen the unsigned threat, written in emerald ink, that someone had tacked to Lady Elthea's door the night before the first fire. "So I say we strike back at them at once."

"No," Lady Elthea said. "I don't want—"

Pivor ignored her. "A lot of them drink at The Honeycomb. We can lie in wait in the alley that runs—"

"That's a bad idea, I said. "My gut tells me that not all the Peregrines are involved in this. We need to identify the ones who are. Indiscriminate slaughter would only compound our difficulties."

"If we kill enough of them, the ones who remain will be afraid to send the spirit out again."

"No, they won't," I said. "They'll merely seek to butcher you in turn."

Pivor's lip curled. "I heard that when you founded your fencing academy, you swore your days as a mercenary were over."

"You heard correctly," I said. "Twenty-five years of soldiering was enough. Unfortunately, I have a penchant for losing horses and needy friends. When the combination depletes my coffers, I accept commissions of a certain sort. Pray tell, why are we discussing this?"

"I was just conjecturing that you gave up the mercenary life because you've turned coward. For truly, you seem afraid to fight."

No doubt he said it to shame me into supporting his strategy. But of course there was only one proper response to such an insult, and that wasn't it. Simply because Jarnac was near me, I turned to him. "Sir. Would you do me the honor of acting as my second?"

One of Pivor's friends said, "That figures. One baseborn fellow looks to the other."

Jarnac colored. "It would be better if you asked someone else, Master Selden, because I agree with Pivor. Not in his assessment of your character," he added hastily, "but about what's best to do. We shouldn't waste time trying to ferret out one man from the mass of our foes. We should wage war on them all."

Balin, one of my more promising students, said, "I'll stand for you, Master Selden."

"Thank you," I said. I gave Pivor my best killer's glare. "Then perhaps we can arrange this straightaway."

I'll give him credit, I couldn't stare him down, but he grew pale, no doubt in belated remembrance of my reputation. "Verrano, will you act for me?" he stammered.

"Stop this!" Lady Elthea said. "Didn't you all come here for the same purpose? To succor a poor old woman who needs your help desperately? Then I beg you, please, don't fight among yourselves!"

This time, Pivor chose to heed her. "You're right, of course. Moreover, this is your affair, and if you think this man should be in charge, so be it." He bowed to me. "Master Selden, for my grandaunt's sake, I apologize."

I bowed back. "And for her sake, I accept."

"If we aren't going to massacre the Peregrines, what are we going to do?" Draydech asked.

"The gentlemen of the Lynxes will keep guarding my lady's properties," I said. "Perhaps one of them will spot our human foe, lurking about the scene. You'll try to devise a magic that will locate the salamander. I'll nose around and see what I can uncover through more mundane channels. And by working together, we'll put an end to this outrage." I wished I were as confident as I was trying to sound.

*

I contrived to approach the house from the rear, then hid behind the stable. After a while, a maid trudged out the back door and started tossing feed to the chickens. The birds were plump and lively; she, thin and lethargic. Their feathers shone white in the morning sunlight, while her gown was drab and threadbare. In short, they looked better cared for than she was.

Which was more or less what I'd expected. Her employer was famous for the sumptuous banquets he gave for his fellow Green Peregrines, but, provided one talked to the poor as well as the prosperous, equally notorious for his miserly treatment of his servants.

I checked the windows of the four-story dwelling, making sure no one was peering out, then stepped from concealment. "Hello," I said.

The girl jumped. "Who are you?"

"A friend." I showed her the silver coin in my hand. "With a proposition."

She looked yearningly at the money, reminding me fleetingly of Draydech. But then she scowled and said, "I'm not that kind."

"You mistake me," I said. "I just want to ask you some questions, about things you may have noticed or overheard. Though I must admit, there's a chance that something you say could embarrass your master. So I'll understand if you decline."

She glanced over her shoulder at the house, then snatched the coin. "What do you want to know?"

*

The racket in The Honeycomb was deafening. The tavern was packed, most of the patrons were roaring drunk, and two lunatics were playing bagpipes. We lads at the corner table had to bellow with the rest to make ourselves heard.

"And that was that," said one of my companions, a burly hire-sword with a forked beard, a broken nose, and a Green Peregrine favor pinned to the sheepskin collar of his jacket. "When they saw that, armed only with a soup ladle, I'd killed eight of their band in half as many seconds, the rest of the bastards turned tail."

"Amazing," I said. I was trying to sound admiring, and truly, I was impressed by his powers of invention. I stroked my false whiskers the way I always do when I wear them, to make sure they aren't falling off. "Of course, if what we hear in the City of Silks is true, it's no wonder you men of Balathex are master warriors. Folk say you keep in constant practice fighting one another. For instance, you Peregrines are at odds with the Leopards, isn't that so?"

"The Snow Lynxes," someone corrected.

"Pardon me, the Snow Lynxes. What's that all about, anyway? And who's winning?"

Smiling slyly, the fellow with the broken nose said, "I'm afraid that's a very long story. And my throat's already parched."

Taking the hint, I waved for the barkeep to bring another jug.

*

Lithe and lightning-quick, Marissa flowed through the gloomy practice hall, a dagger flashing in either hand and her short black hair flying about her head. When she finished the exercise, I said, "Your high guard is a hair too high."

"Says you," she replied. If she'd kept to her usual schedule, she'd been practicing hard for an hour, but she wasn't even slightly winded. "Good evening, Selden. Stop by to sign up for some lessons?"

"Who could afford your rates?" I said, sauntering from the doorway into the hall. "Well, perhaps I could if I could stay away from the hippodrome, but that's by the by. I need information about the Green Peregrines."

She shrugged. "I don't belong to any faction, any more than you do."

"But most of the Peregrines who study swordplay do so under you, just as the majority of the Snow Lynxes train with me. I know you hear things."

"Suppose I do. Why would I betray my students' confidences to the likes of you?"

"To prevent a full-scale blood-feud. To keep the city from burning down. Either one would be bad for trade."

She smiled crookedly. "Why not say, to keep the sun from turning to dung while you're at it? You'll have to do better than prophecies of doom."

I put my hand on my purse. "How much do you want?"

"At present, I don't need money. It's been a good year. But is it true that you learned sword-and-cape fighting up north?"

I winced. A fencing master needs to hold onto a few martial secrets if he hopes to shine among his rivals. "You're a blood-sucking bitch, Marissa. You know that, don't you?" I unfastened my cloak. "All right, grab a wrap and a longer blade, and I'll give you a lesson."

*

And so it went. As myself or in disguise, I roamed the city, gossiping, flattering, cajoling, bribing, and occasionally threatening. Questing for information. Coming up empty. Meanwhile, Lady. Elthea lost a lumberyard and a warehouse full of bolts of linen. The latter fire spread to a pair of tenements belonging to an inoffensive gentleman of the insignificant Gray Steels. Another thirteen people died.

Finally, reluctantly, I went to my employer's home to describe my lack of progress.

*

This time the council of war convened in Lady Elthea's bedchamber, a high-ceilinged dimly lit room hung with somber tapestries. Though clean, it smelled of her long illness. She lay in a canopy bed, her shoulders propped by a mound of pillows. She seemed even gaunter and frailer than the last time I'd seen her, as if some of her strength had burned along with her properties. Jarnac sat on a stool beside her, holding her hand. He looked haggard, too. Evidently the nights of futile, sleepless sentinel duty were wearing him down.

"All I'm certain of," I said, concluding my dismal excuse for a report, "is that there's no grand conspiracy among the Green Peregrines. When they discuss striking at you Snow Lynxes, they talk about maneuvers in Council, sharp business practice, and the occasional duel, not magic and arson. Indeed, most of them would never even consider a tactic that could endanger the entire town. More than ever, I'm convinced that we're up against one man, acting without the knowledge of his fellows. Unfortunately, I still don't know who he is."

"And I still can't find the salamander," Draydech said morosely. "It ought to light up the psychic landscape like a bonfire. Even if they're sending it back to its own plane after every chore—and that's unlikely, given the amount of energy required—I should be able to sense the opening and closing of the gate. And yet ..." He spread his pudgy hands.

"Still, we're grateful to you gentlemen for your efforts," said Pivor with leaden sarcasm. He turned to his grandaunt. "Now can we try my plan? If we just keep bleeding Peregrines, we're bound to come to the fire-starter eventually."

"No," said Lady Elthea with unexpected firmness. "I'd rather burn in this bed, if it comes to that, than send you into the streets to slaughter people at random."

"But we can't bear to see you hurt any further," Jarnac told her.

"No," Lady Elthea repeated. "I forbid it. There has to be a better way."

"As a matter of fact," I said, "I'm not done yet. I began by making inquiries about the Green Peregrines rather than Balathex's community of sorcerers because the latter are proverbially closemouthed. But now it's time to look at them. After all, one of them had to conjure the spook. The question is, which?"

"Probably one of the Peregrine household mages," said Pivor impatiently. "Or if not, any one of a host of free lances."

"No," said Draydech thoughtfully. "The sorcerers hereabouts aren't saints. In truth, a few are scoundrels. Still, we have an understanding. Certain tacit, self-imposed prohibitions. Now that I think about it, I don't believe that anyone I know would unleash a salamander inside the city walls."

"Then our man is a clandestine practitioner," said I, my pulse ticking faster. "A rogue neither your fraternity nor the authorities would tolerate if they did know about him. We can conjecture that he generally sells his services to criminals. That he lives in a bad part of town. That he hasn't been here long, or you would at least have heard rumors of his presence."

"You're about to propose another search, aren't you?" Jarnac said. "Well, I for one don't see the point. You've already turned the city upside down."

"But this time, I'll have a clearer image of what I'm hunting," I said. "Trust me, that makes a difference."

Lady Elthea said, "I believe Master Selden can find the wretch. Let's let him try."

"Grandaunt," Pivor said, "you have to understand. Devoted as we all are to your wishes and your welfare, this affair encompasses other issues. If an insult to you goes unavenged for any length of time, that reflects on the honor of all the Snow Lynxes. And if we can't find a specific culprit to punish, it's better to chastise all the Green Peregrines than do nothing. Selden can search if you want him to, but we're not going to wait on the result."

"Year in and year out, I've watched this stupid feud claim too many lives," Lady Elthea said. "I won't to be the cause of it flaring up again. Please, child, hold off. I'm dying, you know. This is likely the last favor I'll ever ask of you."

Pivor grimaced. "Very well. I'll give Selden until midnight tomorrow. After that, the Blues will take to the streets and settle matters our way."

"Fair enough," I said. I turned to Draydech. "Finish your wine and come on. If I'm going to stalk a mage, I want you with me."

*

There's a part of Balathex, the Whispering City, the City of Fountains, we call the Dry Quarter, where the fountains abundant elsewhere are few and far between, the streets narrow to twisting alleys, and the cobbles turn to muck beneath one's feet. When the City Guards patrol the area, which is seldom, they go in twos and threes, and as often as not, ignore the screams that ring from the shadowed courtyards.

Draydech and I had been prowling this warren since our departure from Lady Elthea's mansion the previous evening. A weary ache in my joints attested to the fact that it was harder for me to do without sleep than it used to be.

Still, I was in good spirits. Peering up at the narrow strip of sky visible between the steeply pitched rooftops, gauging the position of the waning moon, I judged that I had three hours till midnight. Time enough to forestall Pivor's assault if, as I hoped, I was about to net my quarry.

I pointed at a sagging post-and-beam tenement. It had a cobbler's shop and a bakery on the ground floor, apartments above. "If the kidnapper spoke true, that's the place. Can you sense anything?"

Draydech squinted. After a moment, he said, "Yes. The top story has a nasty sheen to it. Someone's worked magic up there, some of it involving torture, sacrifice, and the Abyss."

"Sounds like our lad," I said. "Is he at home?"

"I can't say. The residue of his sorcery masks any other impressions."

"Well, there's an easy way to find out. Come on." We slunk up the street, through a doorway that stank of urine, and up four creaky flights of stairs.

I didn't see any point in giving the man we were after a chance to ready a spell. I drew my sword and kicked his door. It flew open and I rushed through.

My violent entry served no purpose. The warlock was home, but in no condition to harm me. A bald, hook-nosed man in a hooded robe, he lay sprawled on a dark stain in the middle of the floor. The reek of feces filled the air.

I knelt beside him, and, examining him by the wan light that spilled through the open shutters, found a narrow slit on each side of his throat. I tried to flex his cool, waxy-looking arm. It resisted, but it bent.

Behind me, Draydech muttered an incantation. A globe of sickly green foxfire appeared in the air. Its glow revealed that the one-room apartment had been ransacked. A chest stood open, and clothing lay scattered across the floor. Codices and pieces of parchment were strewn about.

"Damn!" said Draydech. "The Luck Lords hate us! Damn, damn, damn!" He kicked a stool across the floor.

Grasping at straws, I said, "Can we be certain that this man is the mage?"

"Yes. I can tell from the lingering traces of his aura."

"Shit," I said. "Well, perhaps it isn't all bad. If the bastard's dead, he can't lead us to his employer. But on the other hand, if the magician's gone, the salamander's gone, so at least we don't have to worry about the town burning down. Right?"

"Wrong. The creature's probably still around. No reason it shouldn't be. I suspect the mage commanded it to obey his patron. Otherwise, Balathex would already be in flames. But without the wizard's power bolstering the Green Peregrine's control, the elemental could slip its reins at any time. The threat of a conflagration is actually greater than before."

"Wonderful," I growled, rising. "We'd better search this place ourselves. I don't know what the murderer was looking for, but—"

"Watch out!" Draydech cried. To this day, I don't know what he could have seen or heard that I missed; it must have been his mystical senses that alerted him. He sprang at me and knocked me away from the window.

An instant later, there was a quarrel in his back. He tried to speak and then he was gone, just like that, death's ghastly conjuring trick that stuns and appalls no matter how many times one sees it played on a friend.

Fortunately, though my thoughts were frozen, my reflexes weren't. I threw myself to the floor. Another bolt whizzed through the air above me.

The marksman, who must be shooting from the window directly across the street, had had at least two crossbows loaded and ready.

I didn't see much reason to stand back up and find out if he had a third. It would be wiser to slip out of the apartment. I crawled to the door.

Onrushing footsteps clattered up the stairs. The crossbowman's colleagues, without a doubt. It sounded as if there were half a dozen. Long odds even for a fencing master, especially if one had to worry about taking a quarrel in the back while one fought.

I wished I could lock the door. That might at least buy me a few seconds. But, cunning fellow that I was, I'd broken the latch. And as long as I was taking stock of my ill fortune, it was a pity I was too high to leap from the window to the street. If I tried to climb down the wall, the marksman would shoot me for certain.

I crawled back to the window, pulled off my cloak, stuck it on the end of my sword, and raised it. Another bolt thrummed overhead. Instantly, discarding the makeshift lure, I scrambled up onto the windowsill and leaped.

Though the street was narrow, it was an awkward jump, and I didn't land gracefully. I slammed down on my belly on the marksman's windowsill, half in and half out, legs dangling. My attacker, a skinny, coppery bearded fellow, smashed an arbalest over my head.

For a moment, I blacked out. When I came to, he was pushing me backward.

I grabbed the windowsill with one hand and whipped out my dagger with the other. I thrust. The blade scraped a rib, then plunged deep into the marksman's chest. He groaned and flopped on top of me.

I shoved him off, then hauled myself into the empty apartment he'd been shooting from. When I examined him, I saw that Draydrech was avenged.

My knees were weak, my crown throbbed, and blood trickled down my forehead. I wanted to sit and rest, but I knew I mustn't give my remaining assailants a chance to figure out where I'd gone and tree me again. I dragged my dagger out of the redhead's breast, then hurried out the door.

*

By the time I reached Lady Elthea's mansion, I felt a little better. Perhaps in recognition of the noblewoman's disapproval, Pivor's miniature army, if one cared to dignify it with that name, was awaiting midnight outside in her garden. He'd gathered about a hundred men, those who'd stood watch over his kinswoman's holdings plus some new recruits. Casks of ale and wine sat on trestles beside a dry fountain, and the cool night air smelled of drink.

Working my way through the throng, I spotted Pivor drinking from a tankard. "Good evening," I hailed him.

He pivoted. Squinted. "You're hurt."

"A scratch," I said. "You can send the mob home."

He frowned. "Are you saying you found the magician?"

"More or less. I'm sure you can appreciate that no one should hear my tidings before my employer." I waved down a passing footman. "Please tell your mistress Selden is here."

I thought he'd return and usher me into her presence, but instead, leaning heavily on a gleaming staff, she hobbled out onto the marble steps beneath the porte cochere. At her appearance, a hush settled over the crowd.

I bowed. "My lady, I know your enemy's name." The Snow Lynx blades jabbered excitedly. "I deduced it just a short while ago. Truth to tell, I should have realized before, but I'm like everyone else in Balathex. I'm so wearily familiar with the enmity between Snow Lynx and Green Peregrine that it was difficult to think beyond it."

Pivor gaped at me. "Are you saying the incendiary isn't a Peregrine? What about the threat?"

"Anyone can buy green ink. The letter was merely a ruse to divert suspicion from the real culprit. Think about it: Lady Elthea isn't active in public life. Even her late husband didn't make himself any more obnoxious to the Peregrines than many another member of your faction. Why, then, would a Peregrine choose to persecute her and her alone of all your number? Wouldn't it make more sense to attack a genuine Snow Lynx leader such as you?"

Pivor opened his mouth, then closed it again.

"While you ponder that, I continued, "you can chew on this as well. Lady Elthea, we all worried that you would indeed burn in your bed, but in point of fact, the salamander never came here. Instead, it devoted its attentions to your commercial ventures. Once again, if your foe intends your destruction, one has to wonder why.

"Here's what I think. You have a wealthy friend. Like me, he started common and shinned his way up into the lesser gentry. Unlike me, he yearns to rise higher still. In Balathex, that isn't easy, so he decided to ruin you, then offer to cover your losses if you'd adopt him. Or perhaps he wouldn't have been so crude; he might have relied on your gratitude. Either way, he expected to gain a title and membership in one of the Ancient Kindreds." I turned. "Isn't that right, Master Jarnac?"

Jarnac glared at me. "This is absurd."

"Is it? Once we started standing watch, every building that caught fire did so while you were guarding it. Moreover, Draydech and I found the mage who conjured the salamander slain. By a thrust from a thin blade like yours. No Green knew we were hunting the warlock, but you did. You were here when we hatched the plan. Since the man could identify you, you got to him first, silenced him, and ransacked his quarters to make sure that he hadn't written your name down anywhere. Afterwards, you found you were still afraid. Maybe you were worried that your search had missed something or that Draydech's sorcery could make a dead man speak. In any event, you hired a band of assassins to lie in wait for us. Perhaps, in the moments of life remaining to you, it will console you to know that only I escaped."

Pivor said, "Hold on. How do you know that the fire wizard died after you left here yesterday?"

"As a corpse cools, it stiffens," I replied. "But after the better part of a day, it starts to go limp again. The body was at that stage when I found it."

Jarnac's forehead glistened with sweat. His voice breaking, he said, "You can't prove a single thing against me."

"True," I said. "Not to the satisfaction of a court of law. But I don't have to. I've cast aspersions on your honor, and you're supposed to call me out. If you don't, I'll challenge you, and you'll still have to fight. It's time you learned there are disadvantages to being an aristocrat."

He turned. "Lady Elthea, I swear—"

Her old eyes glittered. "You vile thing."

Jarnac's face crumpled. "All right. I confess. I surrender. Send for the City Guards."

I couldn't help feeling disappointed. Though I was confident that the authorities would behead him in due course, I wanted to kill him myself. But I also figured we needed him alive for the nonce, to help us deal with the salamander. "Tell us about the elemental," I said.

"As you wish, " he said. He opened his collar and pulled out a round brass medallion on a chain. "This will be the true consolation, getting rid of the beast." He lifted the chain over his head. "You can't imagine how it's been. I didn't mean to harm anyone. But the thing kept pushing and squirming—"

His sandy hair burst into flame.

An instant later, fire blazed out of his eye sockets and silently screaming mouth. His skin shone dazzling white, like molten metal, and wisps of blackened cloth flew away from his body. Crying out in shock and terror, the men around him recoiled. For a moment, he reeled about in manifest agony, then dropped into a truculent crouch.

At last, too late, I understood why Draydech had never been able to find the spirit. Its summoner had somehow hidden it inside Jarnac. And now, seizing control, it had transmuted their mingled substance into something more nearly resembling its native form.

I drew my dagger and lunged. Heat seared me. My point plunged into the salamander's breast. Seemingly unhurt, it lifted one fiery hand to seize me.

I sidestepped its grab and slashed at its other hand. The dagger snagged the chain, and I ripped it out of the elemental 's grasp.

Evidently, it had been a good idea, because the salamander snarled and tried to snatch the medallion back. I surmised that in the hands of a mage, it might have the power to subdue the creature.

Wishing that I were a sorcerer, wincing at the blistering touch of the metal, I gripped the chain securely in my fist, wheeled, and ran. The panicky Snow Lynxes parted before me, clearing my path to the street. The salamander lumbered in pursuit.

After a few steps, it became apparent that the creature couldn't catch me. Perhaps it would have been slow in any world, in any form, but more likely it was clumsy using Jarnac's legs. Foolishly, I imagined that for the next little while, my primary problem might be making sure that it didn't abandon the chase.

The air around me grew warmer. I glanced back, but the salamander, now entirely enveloped in a corona of hissing blue flame, was still several yards back. For another heartbeat, I still failed to grasp what was happening. Then I remembered how the spirit had kindled fire at a distance, simply by willing it.

I dodged, an instant too late. The blast hurled me through the air and smashed me down on the cobbles. Though stunned, I started to scramble up, then noticed that my left sleeve was on fire. I rolled over and over till the blaze went out, then jumped to my feet and dashed on.

From then on, my progress was a nightmare. Explosions blinded and deafened me. Gasps of hot air charred my throat. By zigzagging, I managed to prevent the salamander from centering a blast on me, but only at the cost of eroding my lead. All things considered, I was reasonably certain that I'd never reach my destination.

But I was wrong. Eventually I staggered around a corner and there it was, the ground on which I'd chosen to make my stand. I ran a few more feet, drawing the salamander to where I wanted it. Then I sucked in a deep breath, spun and charged.

Perhaps the maneuver surprised it, because it didn't even try to get out of my way. I grappled it and bulled it backward. It wrapped its blazing arms around me.

The next moment seemed to last an eternity. I felt my skin crisping, my tunic, breeches, and eyebrows catching fire. Then the salamander and I plunged off the riverbank.

As I'd prayed, the elemental's halo of flame went out when we splashed into the stream. But its flesh was still hot. The water around it started to boil. I imagined that in time it could cook me like a crayfish.

But now that I had the elemental submerged, I wasn't about to give it a chance to come up for air. Clinging to it, I stabbed it again and again. As far as I could tell, these new wounds didn't trouble it either. Meanwhile, it tried to thrust me away.

Though no one could have seen much in the dark water, I still sensed my vision fading. My ears rang and my chest ached, the compulsion to gulp a breath becoming insupportable.

And then the salamander stopped struggling. Its body turned soft, crumbled and dissolved in the current, as if it had burned itself to ash.

I dropped the knife and amulet, then, with the dregs of my strength, floundered to the surface. After filling my lungs several times, I paddled to the shore, only to discover that my arms were too feeble to drag me out of the river.

Gauntleted hands gripped my wrists and hauled me onto the grass. "I came after you," Pivor said.

"I'm afraid you missed all the fun," I wheezed. "They're dead, the spook and Jarnac both." I started coughing. I wondered vaguely if it was from swallowing smoke or water.

"You need a physician!"

"That would be nice. Not that I'm dying, but I could definitely use some ointment for my scorched parts. Just let me lie here a minute, and then, I think, I'll be able to walk."

After a pause, Pivor said, "Thank you for bringing us the truth. I keep thinking about things my grandaunt has always said. And all the blood I nearly shed, for nothing. Do you think there might be an honorable way to end the feud? I mean, without killing all the Green Peregrines."

I smiled, which hurt my face. "It's worth considering," I said.

Death in Keenspur House

The living eyed me with emotions ranging from hope to dislike. Mouth agape, eyes wide, smallsword still sheathed at his hip, chest hacked to bloody ruin, the corpse stared up at the high ceiling with its painted scene of nymphs and deer. I stooped to see if his eyes still held the image of the man who'd cut him down. They didn't. That trick has never worked for me, nor, so far as I know, for anyone.

Stout and balding, a man in his middle years like myself, Lord Baltes asked, "Are you learning anything, Master Selden?"

I straightened up. "It's too early to say."

Lanky and sharp-featured like so many members of the Keenspurs, Tregan snorted. "Surely it's clear enough what happened. Venwell had the bad luck to blunder into the thief, who then had to kill him to make his escape."

"Is that what your magic reveals?" I asked. A talent for wizardry ran in the Keenspur blood, and in addition to serving as his brother Baltes's lieutenant, Tregan was the household mage.

His mouth twisted. "No, actually. The signs are muddled. But it's common sense, surely."

"Maybe," I said, inspecting a floral tapestry spoiled by eight long rust-brown streaks. The murderer had evidently used it to give his weapon a thorough wiping. "I'd like to see the room where the wedding gifts are on display."

"What will that accomplish?" asked the sorcerer. "The killer took the ruby tiara. It isn't there for you to examine anymore. We sent for you because Marissa claims you know your way around the stews and thieves' dens down in the Dry Quarter. You should be hurrying there—"

"You sent for him because he's the one who caught the salamander and so kept the city from burning down, or the Green Peregrines and Snow Lynxes from slaughtering one another," Marissa said. Lithe and long-legged, she'd been the principal fencing master to the Peregrine faction as I was for the Lynxes. "He has a knack for puzzling things out."

"I hope so." Baltes waved his hand. "The room is this way." Tregan, Marissa, and I followed him, and an assortment of his kinsmen and servants traipsed along after us.

The remaining gifts—begemmed goblets, gold plates and trays, rings, bracelets, armor, glazed jars of spice and unguents, furs, and bolts of velvet and silk—glowed in the candlelight. Relatives, political allies, and trading partners had sent presents from as far away as Yanla.

I'd walked a warrior's path my whole life long, first as a mercenary, then, primarily, as a master-of-arms, though I still occasionally rented out my blade if the job didn't require actually riding off to war. So perhaps it was no surprise a splendidly crafted broadsword, with emeralds gleaming in the hilt and scabbard, caught my eye. I hankered to pick it up and try a cut or two, but that would have been gauche and inappropriate.

So I kept my mind on the task at hand, wandered about, inspected the heaps of gleaming treasure, and tried to think of something useful. "Are we certain," I asked, "that only the tiara is missing?"

"Yes," Baltes said.

"I need to confer with my colleague," I said. "We'll only be a moment." Conscious once more of the animus with which so many of Baltes's people regarded me, I led Marissa into the next room.

"What have you figured out?" she whispered, brushing back a strand of her short black hair.

"Nothing for certain."

"Curse it, Selden, I'm the one who urged them to send for you. Don't make me look a fool."

"Believe me," I said, "I want to unmask the killer and recover the bauble as much as you do, and not just because Baltes will reward me. To lay the feuds to rest for good."

For years, the nobles of Balathex had divided themselves into factions. Each of the five disliked the others, but the Green Peregrines and Snow Lynxes, the most powerful, detested one another with extraordinary virulence. When the fire elemental's depredations fanned their mutual hatred and suspicion, their enmity nearly plunged the city into outright civil war.

Strangely enough, that turned out to be a good thing, because it threw a scare into every noble with a particle of sense. In the aftermath, Pivor, a leader of the Snow Lynxes, led a campaign to quell the factions. The forthcoming wedding represented the culmination of his efforts. When Baltes, a widower, married his youngest daughter Lukinda, it ought to lay the rivalries to rest for good and all.

But only if the wedding came off as planned. On the surface, there was no reason why the murder and burglary, no matter how unfortunate, need prevent it. But my gut warned me that, if left unresolved, such an alarming, inexplicable calamity could bring the old malice and mistrust creeping back.

"So," said Marissa, "what did you want to talk about?"

"First, tell me about Venwell. Did you train him?"

"Yes."

"Was he an able, seasoned swordsman?"

"Very much so."

I sighed. "I was afraid of that. Now I need to know how hard I can push these folk. I have things to say they won't like. I won't mean to asperse their honor, but some may take it that way."

She snorted. "Wonderful. Because they don't like you." Understandably so, I supposed, since for years, I made my living teaching Lynxes how to kill them. "I don't know that you dare push them very hard at all."

"Damn it, I have to do the job they brought me here to do. Will you back me up?"

She made a sour face. "Well, I did get you into this, even if I'm starting to regret it."

"Let's rejoin the others."

"What do you have to tell us?" Baltes asked.

"Milord," I said, "I'm no sage—far from it—but as Marissa told you, sometimes I have an eye for what's odd about a particular situation. We have several oddities here. For starters, neither the sentries nor the watchdogs outside detected an intruder, nor have we found any sign of forced entry."

"What of it?" Tregan asked. "As I understand it, there are thieves skillful enough to sneak into any house."

"Perhaps," I said. "But consider this, also. Venwell died of cuts to the chest. He saw his killer. Yet he perished without even trying to draw his blade."

"Perhaps," Tregan said, "he froze."

Marissa shook her head. "No. I schooled him too well."

"It's possible," I said, feeling as if I were about to dive from a cliff, "he knew his slayer. If it was someone he trusted, that would explain why he took no alarm until it was too late, even though the killer had a naked sword in his hand. Similarly, if the culprit was someone who lives here in the mansion—or is currently a guest—he wouldn't need to sneak past the guards and hounds, or break open a window or door."

For a moment, everyone just gawked at me. Then a footman said, "But everybody liked Venwell."

"That may be," I replied, "but a thief still couldn't afford to let him report that he'd seen him stealing the tiara."

"Ridiculous," Tregan spat. "Ours is a wealthy and honorable house. No one here would steal the gift."

"Not even a servant?" I asked. "Or the least of your kin, perhaps burdened with gambling debts?"

"No," Tregan said, "I don't believe it."

"Have you wondered," I said, "why the thief took only a single article? A housebreaker could surely have carried away more. But if the murderer never left, if he needed to hide his plunder here in the mansion for the time being, he might have reckoned that the more he stole, the harder it would be to conceal. Or, if he's a member of the household, it might have shamed him to take more than he reckoned he truly needed."

Skinny and sharp-nosed like Tregan but younger, a Keenspur named Dremloc stepped forth from the mass of observers and planted himself in front of me. Here it comes, I thought. At least it looked as if he meant to deliver a formal challenge. I had a fair chance of surviving that, as I wouldn't if he and all his outraged relations simply assailed me in a pack.

"You Snow Lynx bastard," he said. "I say you're a lia—"

But just before he could articulate that unforgivable word, Marissa sprang between us. She glared into his eyes, and he flinched. Since she'd trained him, he knew how deadly a combatant she was, and accordingly feared her more than he did me.

"Master Selden," she said, "is under my protection. Is that clear?"

Dremloc scowled, but also inclined his head.

Baltes turned to me. "Do you have more to say?" he asked.

I had a nagging sense that I should. That I'd missed things a sharper eye and brain might have discerned. But it would have only have undermined his confidence in me to say so. "You've heard my conjectures, Milord. They point to an obvious course of action. Search the mansion, find the tiara, and hope its hiding place reveals who took it."

The assembly growled at the prospect of having their quarters and belongings ransacked. Tregan said, "Ridiculous." Evidently it was a favorite word of his.

"No," Baltes said, "it isn't. Master Selden's guesses are only that, but they seem plausible. We will search the house, if only to lay the suspicions he's roused to rest, and you, brother, will try once again to locate the tiara with your sorcery."

We organized ourselves into search parties and formulated a plan. I cast a final admiring glance at the broadsword with the emeralds in its hilt, then set forth with my companions.

The Keenspur mansion was enormous. It took well into the morning to complete our search, and even so, we didn't look everywhere. Some hiding places simply seemed too unlikely to bother with, and I wasn't bold enough to suggest that we rummage through Baltes's or Tregan's apartments, even if I'd believed it would serve a purpose.

Our mundane search failed to produce the tiara, nor did Tregan's divinations fare any better. At the end of it all, standing before Baltes, the magician, and their tired, irritated relations and retainers, I did indeed feel "ridiculous."

"I'm sorry, Milord," I said. "I thought I'd reasoned my way to the truth, or a part of it anyway, but it appears I was mistaken."

Tregan sneered. "Will you now make inquiries among the robbers and knaves, as we told you to in the first place?"

"Yes, Milord." I certainly had no better plan.

As I walked to the door with as much dignity as I could muster, I heard Dremloc and another young blade muttering in my wake. "This is like sending a weasel to escort the chickens safely into the coop," my would-be challenger said.

"What do you mean?" his companion asked.

"I don't claim to understand any of this, why the tiara was taken or Venwell had to die. But you can bet your last copper a Lynx is responsible."

The seed of suspicion was already sprouting.

For the next week, I went about mostly in disguise, in the costumes of other lands or with false whiskers gummed to my chin, prowling all night and sleeping by day. Reasoning it would be difficult for a woman to wear the tiara in Balathex, I began my investigations among receivers of stolen goods who specialized in moving them safely out of town. When that availed me nothing, I moved on to the commoner sort of thieves' market, and bribed whores and tavern keepers to tell if any of the city's more accomplished housebreakers had lately boasted of a coup, started spending lavishly, or was lying low to avoid hunters like myself. That was of no use, either. If any of the city's rascals had knowledge of the tiara, it would take a shrewder, subtler agent than me to tease out the information.

Meanwhile, Balathex commenced a slide back into the hateful, bloody days of yore. Hotheaded young Keenspurs started wearing Green Peregrine tokens, their friends from other houses followed suit, and the fools among the supposedly defunct Snow Lynxes would have felt cowardly had they not responded by displaying their own badges. Soon the Gray Steels, Crimson Orchids, and Sons of the Comet took up the old practice, too. From there, it was a short step to insults, mockery, and scuffles in the street.

Baltes, Tregan, Pivor, and other leaders of the noble houses did their best to quash the unrest, and at their behest, the City Guards assisted. Thanks to their efforts, the quarrels among the resurgent Snow Lynxes and Green Peregrines, and members of the lesser factions, ended short of grievous harm to any of the principals. But it was only a matter of time before our luck ran out, and I feared that as soon as it did, the blood-feuds would resume in earnest.

All because a crime that, on the surface, had nothing to do with the grudges and rivalries of old. It was perverse, mad, yet it was happening.

In due course, I trudged back to Keenspur House to report my lack of progress.

Somewhat to my surprise, when a lackey admitted me to confer with Tregan and Baltes, I found the latter wearing the broadsword from the wedding gifts. It was contrary to custom to put such a present to use prior to the nuptials, but I could understand why he'd succumbed to the temptation.

I explained what I'd accomplished, or rather, what I hadn't. It didn't take long, as accounts of failure rarely do, so long as a man resists the urge to make excuses.

"I'm beginning to think," said Tregan, sneering, "that your success in catching the salamander was a fluke."

I was starting to wonder myself, but still had enough pride left to resent his contempt. "Should I infer, Milord, that your efforts to solve our problem with wizardry have proved as futile as my own?"

The question made him glare.

"Tell me the truth," Baltes said. "Is there any point in your poking around the slums any further?"

I sighed. "I can't be certain, but probably not."

"Then don't. Tell me what I owe you for your time, and the steward will pay you on your way out."

Now that—his assumption that I wasn't merely stymied but defeated—truly stung me, and perhaps it was the injury to my pride that finally goaded my brain into squeezing forth some semblance of a fresh idea.

"Please, Milord," I said. "I don't want your coin, not until I earn it. I have a further course of action to suggest."

He cocked his head. "What?"

"I'd like to take up residence here from now until the wedding."

"Why?"

I didn't know myself, really, but had to improvise some sort of answer. "Maybe if I become more familiar with the murder scene, some new insight will occur to me. Or, failing that, maybe I can at least stop the robber from returning and doing any more harm."

"Nonsense," Tregan snapped. "You're reverting to your first idiot notion, that one of our own family, or loyal retainers, is responsible for the atrocity. You want to spy on us in hope of identifying the culprit."

"No," I said, and wasn't sure if I was lying or not. I was half-way satisfied that none of the household was guilty, yet likewise suspected that some secret awaited discovery within these walls.

"You're aware," Baltes said, "that the old folly of Green Peregrine and Snow Lynx has flared up again. I'm struggling to put the fire out, and I fear your presence here will feed it. You surely won't feel particularly welcome."

"I can tolerate that," I said. "Please, Milord. I want what you and Lord Pivor want, to put the feuds and factions behind us forever. If there's even the slightest chance that my presence here will help accomplish that, or simply lead to the apprehension of Venwell's killer, isn't it worth a try?"

"Perhaps," Baltes said. "Stay for the time being, and we'll see how it goes."

So began my sojourn in Keenspur House. As the head of the family had warned, few of his kin exerted themselves to show me hospitality. It might have been even more unpleasant if I hadn't kept to my nocturnal habits, sleeping the mornings away and roaming the mansion late at night, looking for clues that had eluded me before, trying to imagine what had happened on the night of the murder.

Any huge old pile, no matter how opulent, can turn into a shadowy, echoing, spooky place after the servants turn out the lamps and everyone goes to bed. So it was with the mansion, and perhaps it was that eerie atmosphere that prompted me to recall Venwell's wide eyes and gaping mouth, and to infer what they actually signified.

Marissa was wrong. The lad had frozen. Because he'd faced a supernatural assailant, and any man, no matter how well trained a swordsman, can succumb to terror in such circumstances.

Yet Tregan swore the killing had nothing of the mystical or otherworldly about it, and much as he disliked me, he seemed sincere in his desire to identify the culprit, so what was I to make of that?

I returned again to the suspicion that the thief dwelled within the mansion. I thought of our search, and one area we'd neglected. Because the family kept it locked, Baltes had the only key, and thus it scarcely seemed a likely or convenient hiding place. It was, moreover, the sort of place folk rarely visit by choice.

But, though I still possessed no certainties, merely a collection of vague suspicions and intuitions, I decided I wanted to visit it, or at least inspect the entrance. I found an oil lamp that was still burning, lifted it from its sconce, and set off through the hushed, gloomy chambers and corridors. Portraits, busts, and statues seemed to glower as I passed, and suits of plate armor standing on display looked misshapen as ogres.

Then a pair of figures skulked from the shadows to bar my path.

It was Dremloc and his crony. Each was only half dressed, with feet bare and shirt unlaced. But despite the inadequacy of their attire, they'd taken the trouble to arm themselves. The flickering yellow light of my lamp gleamed on the smallswords in their hands.

"Don't be stupid," I said. "I'm here to help your family, I'm Lord Baltes's guest, and if that's not enough for you, Marissa would take it ill if you harmed me."

They didn't answer, just stalked forward, further into the circle of lamplight, and then I saw what I'd missed before: their eyes were closed.

Happily, I didn't freeze, though I admit a chill oozed up my spine. Retreating, I set the lamp down on a table, drew my broadsword, and yelled for help. The Keenspurs spread out to flank me, then rushed in.

Somnambulism didn't hinder their swordplay. The slender thrusting blades streaked at me, and I dodged and parried frantically, meanwhile striving to keep either of my opponents from working his way around completely behind me.

Even if I'd wanted to kill them, I didn't dare, for fear of their kindred's retaliation. But neither could I simply defend and defend until one of them got lucky and slipped an attack past my guard. I feinted at the crony's face, and he jumped back. His retreat bought me a moment to concentrate solely on Dremloc. I parried his next thrust, feinted high, then made a drawing cut to his knee.

To my relief, the blade sliced his flesh precisely as I'd intended. His leg gave way. I stepped in close and bashed his jaw with my weapon's pommel. Bone cracked. He reeled, dropped, and lay motionless, his trance knocked into true insensibility.

It was then that help finally came rushing into the room, in the persons of Baltes, Tregan, and six of their household guards.

"By the Seven Bright Angels," Baltes said. He wore a robe, nightshirt, and slippers, but, like my assailants, carried a sword—in his case, the sword with the emeralds. "What's happened?"

"Milord," I panted, "I regret this. But I had no choice. Your kinsmen attacked me."

"No," said Dremloc, ashen, voice shaky, clutching at this bloody knee. No longer sleepwalking in any obvious way. "Don't believe him. We found him looking at that jade statuette yonder as if mustering the nerve to pocket it. We told him to leave it alone, and he drew on us."

The fabrication startled me, and it took me a moment to reply. "That isn't so. You and your kinsman were sleepwalking. Possessed, or under some sort of spell. You attacked me."

Despite the pain of his wound, Dremloc managed a laugh. "That's stupid. Wyler and I were drinking and playing at knucklebones in my room. We got hungry, came downstairs to raid the larder, and found this Snow Lynx whoreson looking shifty."

"If that was the reason you left your quarters," I said, "would you have brought your swords? The same influence that controlled you before is tampering with your memory."

Baltes looked to Tregan. "Tell me," the Keenspur leader said, "if there can possibly be any truth to this."

"As you wish," the warlock said. He closed his eyes, murmured under his breath, swept his hands through mystic passes, and swayed from side to side. The darkness flowed and thickened around us, and a bitter taste stung my tongue.

Tregan opened his eyes once more. "There was no magic involved."

"No!" I said. "Somehow, you're mistaken." I pivoted toward Baltes. "Milord, do you truly believe I'd steal from you, when you already offered me gold, and I refused it? Is it likely I'd pick a fight where the odds were against me, in a house full of my adversaries' kin? Or that I'd be the one to cry for help if I did?"

Baltes scowled. "Perhaps it was simply ill will and folly that made the three of you brawl, and no one has the courage to admit it."

"No, Uncle," Dremloc said. "I swear, it happened as I told you."

Meanwhile, I made the corresponding assertion in different words.

"Master Selden," Baltes said, "I suspected no good would come of having you here, and you've proved me right. In other circumstances, I might be inclined to punish you for it. But Pivor and the other Snow Lynxes—former Lynxes, I should say—hold you in esteem, the wedding is only two days hence, and I'm loath to do anything that might stir the old animosities. So just get out."

"Milord," I said, "I was about to follow up on an idea when all this happened. Apparently, our unknown enemy somehow discerned my intent, and used Dremloc and Wyler to stop me. That must mean the notion has something to it. I beg you—"

Baltes's hand clenched on the hilt of his sword. "I've had enough of your foolishness! Go now, or I won't answer for your safety."

I looked at all the Keenspurs and Keenspur servants glaring back at me, and I went.

Afterward, I resolved to put the affair behind me. Since Baltes had discharged me, it was no longer any of my concern, and I'd been lucky to come out of it with my skin intact. But I'd never had much of a knack for minding my own business, and after a morning of moping and grumbling around my school, I went to see Pivor.

He'd already heard I'd disgraced myself among the Keenspurs, but received me anyway, for the sake of the services I'd rendered him in the past. I told him my side of the story, and couldn't judge if he credited it or not.

"I'm glad you escaped unharmed," he said, sitting on a marble bench in the conservatory where he often received callers, if their rank and business was such that formality was unnecessary. Sunlight streamed through the high windows, and the scent of verdure tinged the air. "But you can't let go of it, can you?"

I grinned. "You understand my foibles, Milord."

"Well enough to realize you're here because you want something of me. What?"

"Can you tell me about the early years of the feuding? It was already well underway when I first came to Balathex, and I never bothered to learn the details."

"I don't see the point of your learning them now, but all right. I have time to chat for a bit."

Some of what he told me, I did in fact already know. But eventually the talk turned to a wizard named Yshan Keenspur.

"He was their House mage before Tregan," Pivor said, "from which you can guess that he was an older man. That in turn might lead you to imagine him as a prudent, cool-headed fellow who would try to prevent the rise of the factions, but you'd be wrong. He was one of the instigators, as rabid and bloody-minded a Green Peregrine as ever was. Perhaps he simply had a choleric temperament, or saw it as a way to increase his family's power. Or maybe he dabbled in black magic, and it twisted his mind. There were rumors, but then there always are, whenever a sorcerer is disliked."

"What became of him?" I asked.

"For all his powers, he came to grief in a street brawl, when three Lynxes set on him at once. He died trying to lay a curse on us. But so what? It happened long ago."

"Maybe not long enough." I explained my suspicions, to the extent I understood them myself.

Pivor shook his head. "You realize, the Green Peregrines—the Keenspurs, I mean—would find this allegation even more offensive than anything you've suggested hitherto."

"I suppose."

"On top of that, it doesn't actually explain the theft of the tiara. According to your postulations, the culprit took it to rekindle the hatred between Peregrine and Lynx. But why would anyone anticipate that it would have that result?" He smiled a humorless smile. "Even if, somehow, that's how it's working out."

"I don't know," I said, "but I have figured out what we ought to do next." I told him.

"No," he said at once. "If I insulted Baltes and his kin with such a proposal, it could shatter the peace for good and all."

"Something dangerous is lurking in Keenspur House," I said, "and you're about to send your daughter to live there."

"But not immediately. She'll marry there, but she and Baltes will spend their wedding night, and the following week, at his hunting lodge. Even if your wild hunch is right, that buys us some time. Let's get the bride and groom wed, our two houses, united. Then, perhaps, you and I can broach this matter, if you still deem it necessary."

It was the best he had to offer, so I tried to rest content with it. I failed.

Every great house employs dozens of servants, but when it hosts a wedding, even they aren't enough. The steward, cook, and groundskeeper all have to hire extra help, and accordingly, nobody expects to recognize everyone he sees.

Thus, clad as a common laborer, my grizzled brown hair stained black as Marissa's, my sword, a pry bar, and a lantern hidden in a sack, I found it easy enough to slip back into Keenspur House. I then skulked to the one quiet precinct of the mansion, a chapel where a few votive candles glowed before icons, and stone stairs descended into the earth.

I lit the lantern, strapped on my sword, and headed down. Before long, I came to a door of vertical iron bars. It was locked, but the fact did little to allay my suspicions. Magic that could turn sleeping men into puppets could likely manipulate a lock as well. I broke it with my lever and continued on.

The steps debouched into dank crypts, festooned with webs the spiders spun to snare the beetles, and smelling faintly of incense, embalmer's spice, and rot. The lesser Keenspurs lay behind graven plaques in the walls. The principal lords and ladies had their own private vaults, where stone sarcophagi, the lids often sculpted into likenesses of the occupants, reposed on pedestals in the center.

I assumed Yshan had rated one of the latter, and found him quickly. If his marble likeness could be trusted, he'd possessed the sharp features characteristic of his line, honed beyond the point of gauntness. It gave him a look of fanaticism and spite, which the sculptor had accentuated by rendering him with glaring eyes and a scowl instead of the usual expression of serenity.

I inspected the lid of the sarcophagus, trying to discern whether anyone—or anything—had opened it recently. I couldn't tell. Not unless I opened it myself.

Assuming I could. It looked damnably heavy for a lone man to shift. But I meant to try. I set the lantern down, then, with a dry mouth and sweat starting beneath my arms, tried to work the pry bar into the crack between cover and box. The iron tool scraped the stone.

The lid flew up and to the side, like the cover of a book, straight at me.

It could have shattered my bones, but my reflexes jerked me backward, and perhaps that robbed the impact of some of its force. Even so, the sculpted marble slab slapped me like a giant's hand, knocking me into the wall. I fell, and the lid fell with me, crashing down on top of my legs.

Meanwhile, Yshan, who had, by dint of either magic or prodigious strength, flung his graven image at me, reared up from the sarcophagus. He was relatively intact. The embalmers had evidently done their work well, and his box had protected him from rats and worms. But his face was shriveled, flaking, and streaked with black leakage. His right eye had gone milky, while the left had crumbled inward. A few slimy strings stretched across the vacant socket.

He held a sword, and the glow of the lantern just sufficed to reveal a thick layer of grease coating the blade. When I saw it, I finally comprehended all that had eluded me before.

But I didn't have time to dwell on it. Not with the dead thing stepping out of the coffin, and my legs pinned. I struggled to free myself, and managed to drag my feet out from under the lid.

Just in time. Yshan's sword flashed at my head, and I flung myself out of range. It was the only move that could have saved me, but it put the dead man between me and the doorway. Now, I had no choice but to fight.

I scrambled up and snatched for the sword at my side. Yshan cut at me, and I parried.

The impact jolted my arm, and his weapon nearly smashed through my guard. He was as unnaturally strong as I'd feared.

In other circumstances, wary of his might, I might have fought defensively. But if I hung back, it would give him the chance to cast spells, and I feared that even more than the force of his blows. So I attacked hard whenever I was able.

I drove my point into his chest, but it didn't balk him even for an instant. Why should it, when he was already dead, his vital organs, still and rotting? The only effect was to trap my blade. He whirled a backhand cut at my face. I ducked beneath it and yanked my sword free.

He cut down at my head. Still in a crouch, I just managed to parry, and once again, his stroke nearly hammered through my guard, almost broke my grip on the hilt of my blade.

But not quite, and I discerned that he'd struck with such ferocity as to shift himself off balance. I straightened up, feinted, deceived his awkward attempt at a parry, and slashed his one remaining eye from its socket.

He snarled like a beast, exposing yellow teeth and dark, oozing gums. But he didn't falter as most any mortal creature would
have done. Instead, he struck back immediately, and his aim was
as accurate as before.

As I dodged, I thought, a hit to the vitals hadn't stopped him,
nor had blindness. What if nothing could? I struggled to quash
the panic welling up in my mind.

I opened my guard a hair, praying that he'd think it an error,
not the invitation, the trap, it truly was. That he'd make a particular indirect attack I'd noticed he favored. It seemed likely. It was
a combination well-suited to exploiting the seeming defect in my
defense.

His arm extended, and I immediately stepped forward and to
the side, without waiting to see where his blade was actually going. If I'd guessed wrong, it had an excellent chance of winding
up in my guts.

But I hadn't. He made the move I expected, I avoided it, and
placed myself on his flank in the process, surprising him. Before
he could pivot to threaten me anew, I gripped my hilt with both
hands and cut with all my might.

I didn't quite lop off his sword hand. But I shattered the
wrist bones and left it hanging useless.

Yshan reached to shift his weapon to his off hand, but I
was faster. I beat the greasy blade and knocked the hilt from his
now-feeble grip. The sword clanked on the floor.

Even then, with his terrible strength and resistance to pain
and injury, he might have gotten the better of me if he'd simply
assailed me like a wrestler. But he hesitated, and I cut at his leg.
My sword bit deep, he fell, and I attacked the same spot twice
more, until I was certain I'd done enough damage to keep him
from getting up.

Then I concentrated on his head, driving stroke after stroke
into his skull while avoiding his flailing hand. Finally he collapsed
and lay motionless.

I studied the mangled, seemingly inert carcass for a few heartbeats, then turned and strode toward the exit.

At my back, a harsh voice hissed rhyming words.

The patch of floor beneath me turned to soft muck, treacherous as quicksand. I sank to my knees in an instant, and as I floundered, Yshan began a second incantation, no doubt to finish me off while the ooze held me helpless.

I cast about, spied the open sarcophagus, and tossed my broadsword into it. Then I stretched out my arms, and, straining, succeeded in hooking my fingertips over the lip of the stone receptacle. I heaved with all my strength, and dragged myself up and out of the sucking slime. In the process, I noticed the tiara lying inside the coffin, not that I cared anymore.

I grabbed my sword and leaped at Yshan.

Some shapeless phosphorescent thing was rippling into full existence above him, but it vanished when I cut into his chin and silenced his conjuration. I finished removing his jaw, severed his head, cut the tongue out, and hacked off his fingers. Afterward, I still wasn't certain he was altogether dead, but reasonably confident I'd deprived him of the ability to cast any more spells.

That should have been the end of it. But I hurried back the way I'd come because I feared it wasn't.

Practitioners of black magic don't always pass from the world as easily as normal folk, especially if they leave a dying curse behind. While the feud between the Green Peregrines and Snow Lynxes raged, Yshan had apparently rested easy. But the prospect of peace roused him, and he resolved to avert it.

He had the power to observe things at a distance, and so discerned a sword among the wedding gifts, its blade smeared with grease as such fine weapons generally come from the maker. He decided to switch the sword for the costly one his family had interred with him. Baltes and Lukinda had received such an abundance of presents that it seemed unlikely anyone would notice the substitution.

Yshan emerged from the crypts late one night, had the bad luck to encounter Venwell, and killed him to silence them. He then gave his sword a more thorough cleaning than any common housebreaker, eager to flee, would have done. It couldn't have even a drop of blood on it if it was to pass for a new weapon.

He made the substitution, stole the tiara simply to bolster the impression that an ordinary thief had invaded the mansion, and returned to his vault. In the days that followed, the enchantments he'd laid on the emerald sword began their work. First, a glamour made Baltes yearn to wear the blade without delay. I'd felt the power myself, if only I'd had the wit to realize it. Next, its influence nudged the Keenspurs back toward the rancor of yore.

While through it all, Tregan never sensed supernatural forces at work. Because Yshan had trained him, and held some tricks in reserve. Tricks that allowed him to operate without his successor detecting it.

I doubted he was detecting anything now, either, and that meant I had to get upstairs fast. Because I suspected the warlock's sword had a final trick to play.

The Keenspurs were holding the wedding in their great hall, before hundreds of guests. Lukinda was plump, freckled, and pretty in her gown of shining white, the priest, avuncular in vestments of white and green. Baltes wore the emerald sword. From the looks of it, the ceremony was nearing its conclusion.

"Stop!" I bellowed, starting up the aisle. "Lord Baltes, throw away your sword! It's cursed!"

Everyone turned to gawk at me, and I realized what a peculiar spectacle I must be, clad like a laborer, my legs filthy, a blade in my hand.

Then Dremloc cried, "It's Selden!" The dye in my hair wasn't enough to fool him.

Several of the Keenspurs rose to bar my way. "Get out of here, lunatic," said one, hand on the hilt of his dagger.

"You don't understand," I said.

Nor were they disposed to listen. As they advanced on me, and all the other guests gawked at us, Baltes whipped Yshan's sword from its scabbard and lifted it to threaten his dumbfounded bride.

The priest grabbed his arm, but he shook the man off and shoved him reeling. Nobody else saw, because they were all looking at me, and I could do nothing. The entire length of the hall, and the folk intent on ejecting me or worse, separated me from the altar.

Which meant that despite all my efforts, Baltes would commit the atrocity Yshan had intended. Then the Snow Lynxes would rise up in fury, the Green Peregrines would have no option but to defend themselves, and any nobles who survived this day would prosecute the blood-feud for years to come.

Or so it seemed. But it turned out that someone had heeded my warning after all. Marissa hurled herself at Baltes and grappled with him. She softened him up with a knee to the groin, then twisted his arm. The emerald sword dropped from his fingers.

As soon as it did, he stopped struggling. "Merciful Angels!" he whimpered, his voice full of horror. "Merciful Angels!"

By then, people were finally taking note of what was happening before the altar. I cast about and found Tregan. "The evil's in the blade," I reiterated. "Surely you can sense it now."

He peered at the fallen weapon, then growled, "Yes." He muttered words of power, swept his right hand through a pass, and a ragged darkness swirled up from the sword. People cried out and cringed, but Tregan had the demon, if that was what it was, under control, and it couldn't hurt us. It wailed as it withered away.

Afterward came explanations, and reassurances to the frightened Lukinda and her understandably agitated kin. During the course of it all, Baltes, still white-faced and shaky, told me, "Master Selden, I owe you a hundred apologies. What can I do to make amends?"

I grinned. "Finish the wedding, invite me to the feast, and give me a purse heavy with gold."

Marissa said, "I think I'm due a split."

The Cheat

Falnac was nervous. I could tell by the way he kept swallowing.

I put my hand on the lad's shoulder. "Use what we practiced," I said. "Leap into the distance, feint to the groin, and finish on the outside."

"Yes, Master Selden," he whispered.

"And if the two of you wind up close together, stay there and stab like a madman. Alsagad's taller than you are. Close quarters will make him awkward."

I could have said more, but a swordsman about to fight for his life can only retain so much advice. Indeed, given that this was Falnac's first duel, it was an open question whether he'd remember anything I'd just told him, or anything from his six years of lessons, either.

When they deemed the light sufficient, the seconds called the duelists to a patch of ground where there were no tombstones to trip them up. As they advanced, Dromis caught my eye. He was Alsagad's fencing master as I was Falnac's, and the protocol of dueling required that we treat one another with solemn courtesy. Instead, the big man with the curling mustachios, pointed beard, and hair all dyed a brassy unnatural yellow gave me a sneer, as if to assert that my teaching and my student were so inferior to his that Alsagad's victory was assured.

For a heartbeat, it made me want to see Alsagad stretched out dead on the dewy grass, and then I felt ashamed of myself. Like many quarrels, this one had materialized over a trifle, and any decent man would hope to see if it settled by, at worst, a trifling wound.

The seconds gave the principals the chance to speak words of reconciliation, and of course, being proud young blades of Balathex, they didn't. So Alsagad's second whipped a white kerchief through the air. That was the signal to begin.

The duelists circled one another while waking birds chirped, a cool breeze blew, and dawn stained the river on the far side of the graveyard red. Then Falnac sprang forward.

His blade leaped at Alsagad's crotch in as convincing a feint as I'd ever seen. But the move didn't draw the parry it was meant to elicit. Instead, Alsagad simply cut into Falnac's wrist. Falnac's blade fell from his hand.

The seconds opened their mouths to shout for a halt, but they were too slow. Alsagad slashed Falnac's neck.

Falnac collapsed with blood spurting from the new and fatal wound. Dromis crowed and shook his fist in the air. "Yes!" he bellowed. "Yes! Yes! Yes!"

*

"That murdering little whoreson," I said. I reached to refill my cup and knocked the wine bottle over.

Marissa's scarred, long-fingered hand caught it before it could spill. The close-cropped hair framing her heart-shaped face was inky black in the dim candlelight of the tavern. "You're drunk," she said.

"It was murder!" I insisted.

"If no one had called the halt, then Alsagad was within his rights to keep fighting. And he was a boy, too, wasn't he, no doubt as frightened and frantic as Falnac."

"Don't bet on it. All of Dromis's pupils are arrogant and vicious."

"And yours aren't? Mine are, and thank the gods for it Otherwise, they wouldn't pay good coin to learn to kill."

I shook my head. "There's a difference, and you know it."

"I suppose. By all accounts, Dromis himself is a ruffian, and brutish fencing masters turn out brutish swordsmen. There's no great mystery in it."

"The mystery lies in how they win duel after duel. If you'd seen that feint—"

"Yes, you said it was very pretty."

"Better than pretty. Perfect. Even you would have gone for the parry. But Alsagad didn't."

Marissa sighed. "I admit, I'd love to find out exactly what Dromis teaches that makes his disciples so formidable. Hell, I may need to find out to go earning a living. Students have started leaving me to study with him. I imagine it's happened to you, too."

"Now that you mention it." I took another swig of the tart white wine. "And maybe my students are wise to desert me, if I can't prepare them to defend themselves."

Marissa rested her callused fingertips on the back of my hand. "People die in duels for all sorts of reasons, including sheer bad luck. Falnac's death is sad, but it's no reflection on you."

"It is if Alsagad cheated and I didn't catch him. I'm supposed to be an expert on every aspect of dueling, including treachery and sleights."

"Is that what you think? Dromis is helping his pupils cheat?"

"They win and win and win, don't they, even when facing duelists with more experience. How else can you account for it?"

Marissa took a drink, then wiped her mouth on her sleeve. "I don't know. It's hard to believe that Dromis's system is really so much better than everybody else's. Maestros may claim to know secret invincible techniques—I've done it myself to drum up trade—but you and I know that's mostly rubbish. There are only so many ways to stick a blade in another man's carcass.

"But if Alsagad did cheat," she continued, "I don't see how he could have managed it except by magic, and I assume you were on guard against that."

"Yes." For a moment, reminded of its presence, I felt the round shape of the talisman beneath my shirt. It should have grown hot if Alsagad were carrying a beneficial enchantment on his person or sword, and cold if anyone had cast a curse on Falnac. "Still, I'm not a wizard. It's possible someone slipped something past me." I suddenly waned to be sober, and took a deep breath in a futile attempt to become so. "I'm going to find out."

"Stick your nose into Dromis's business, you mean."

"Yes. If he and Alsaagad conspired to deny Falnac a fair fight, then they truly are murderers according to city law, and I'll see them hang for it."

"Thus mending our fading reputations and drawing our strayed students back to us. I like the idea in principle, and you do have a knack for solving puzzles."

Or at least I'd had some luck at it. Enough that, when people sought my services as a mercenary, a trade I still practiced from time to time to supplement the money I earned teaching, it was often as much for the sharpness of my eyes and wits as the keenness of my blade. "Why do you say you like it in principle?"

"Because I'm sure Dromis is at least as jealous of his secrets as any other maestro. And if his methods empower his students to kill yours, then it's possible they would enable him to do the same to you. So watch your back."

*

I tracked down Olissimal where I should have expected to find him: in the mansion of Falnac's kin. I had no doubt that, supported by his ivory crutches, he'd hovered over the boy's corpse for a long time, ogling the wounds. Now, eyes bright, twisted, stunted leg propped on a leather footstool, he sat in a corner savoring the more rarefied nectar of everyone else's grief.

My mouth and stomach sour from last night's overindulgence, I felt an urge to grab him and drag him out of the room, but of course that wouldn't do. Instead, I paid my respects to Falnac's parents. Who didn't reproach me, unless it was with their eyes.

Afterward, I approached Olissimal with at least a semblance of the courtesy due a scion of one of the Ancient Kindreds. "Master Selden," he said, the corners of his crooked mouth quirking upward, "I didn't expect to see you here today. Come to collect for the boy's lessons?"

I took a breath. "I came to express my sympathy and talk to you."

"Truly?"

"If you'll favor me with a moment of your time."

"I suppose. It's just that you surprise me. You are, after all, the same fellow who called me a degenerate, forbade me to observe the classes at your academy even when I offered to pay, and threatened to whip me if I ever dared watch one of your pupils fighting a duel."

So I had. Many men who are not themselves warriors are interested in the martial disciplines, and generally that's all right. But it had always been plain to me that Olissimal's fascination rose from an underlying thirst to witness killing and mutilation, and while such passive cruelty was relatively harmless, it repulsed me nonetheless.

But now Dromis and his students concerned me more. "Help me," I said, "and I'll lift the ban. You can watch everything but the private lessons." Those were where I passed along my own "secret" techniques, inadequate as they had begun to seem.

"How generous. What sort of help do you require?"

"Nothing difficult. I'm sure you've watched many of the duels Dromis's students have fought. I want you to describe them."

He laughed, startling the mourners and offending against the solemnity of the occasion. "Trying to figure out what makes Dromis's protégés so deadly? Maybe you should have done that before you sent poor little Falnac out to fight one of them."

Once again, I clamped down on my anger. "Will you do it?"

"Oh, why not? After all, there isn't much I enjoy more than chatting about swordplay."

To give him his due, the descriptions were clear and detailed. He was observant and understood dueling as well as a man born with a useless leg ever could. After he finished, I said, "So it's mostly dodging, stop thrusts, and counterattacks. Aggressive responses to the other man's attempt to score. They seldom take the initiative, give ground, or parry."

"Exactly."

"Damn it!" I said. "Only a truly accomplished swordsman can hope to fight that way and get away with it, and even he, only when facing an inferior opponent."

"Yet Dromis's pupils invariably win. Even the novices typically fell their opponents at the end of the first exchange." He smirked as though enjoying my mystification.

"Their success aside," I asked, "do they look like prodigies?"

"No. They display the same defects of stance, balance, guard, and what have you as other students."

"Then..." I groped for a sensible follow-up question. "What about when they brawl in the cockpits and brothels?" Olissimal frequented such places for the same reason he haunted the dueling grounds: he hoped to see men who could walk unaided cut one another to pieces. "Are they similarly successful?"

Olissimal frowned, his gray eyes narrowing. "Now that you mention it, it's a strange thing. Unlike many other young blades, they rarely brawl, even though they're as pugnacious a lot as you'll find in the city. Whenever they give or take offense, they try to steer the dispute in the direction of a formal challenge."

"And what happens when the other fellow insists on drawing on the spot?"

"They don't display their accustomed superiority. Not consistently, at any rate." He cocked his head. "Curious. What do you suppose it means?"

"I don't know yet." I turned and left him to play the vulture.

*

Clad in the nondescript garments he'd borrowed from a servant, the brim of his hat pulled down to shadow his sharp-nosed face, Tregan Keenspur smiled and looked with interest at the bustling life of the street. I realized he was enjoying walking incognito among the common herd like some eccentric prince in a ballad.

That was just as well since I needed him disguised. Dressed in his normal rich attire with lackeys in attendance, a prominent noble and wizard of House Keenspur couldn't go anywhere and do anything without attracting attention. And I didn't want Dromis to learn I was making a study of him.

"That's the school up ahead," I said. "The dark green building with the rust-colored door and shutters."

Tregan cast about. "I need a place to work. I can't cast spells in the middle of the lane without somebody noticing."

"How about there?" I indicated the narrow, shaded gap between two houses. The space was a pace or two removed from the street traffic, yet still afforded a view of the fencing academy.

"That should do," the sorcerer said, so that was where we went.

I kept watch and did my best to shield Tregan's activities from view as he whispered incantations and crooked his fingers into arcane signs. The mystical force accumulating in the air made me feel feverish and sick to my stomach. Then it discharged itself with a soft sound like the pattering of rain.

Tregan put his hand on my shoulder and shifted me aside to get a little closer to Dromis's establishment. The wizard's eyes now glowed with their own inner radiance, but the effect was subtle. No one could have seen it from any distance, not in the daylight, anyway.

He peered for a time, and then said, "The top floor."

"There's something magical there?"

"Yes."

"Is it black magic?" If so, then Dromis's possession of it was a crime in and of itself, and my aristocratic companion was just the man to call him to account for it.

"No. I sense that the enchantment may have served a violent purpose, but it isn't evil as the law defines the term."

I sighed. "Of course not. When were my problems ever solved as easily as that? What is it, then, exactly?"

"I can't say. Not at such a distance, with at least one wall in the way. I'm sorry, Selden. We Keenspurs owe you a considerable debt, and I fear I haven't done all that much to repay it."

"I wouldn't say that." Not out loud, anyway. "At least I know more than I did before."

"But is our discovery relevant? I still don't see how. Dromis may possess some form of magic, but if there were no mystical energies in play when Alsagad killed Falnac, how can the one thing pertain to the other?"

"That's what I have to find out. Now tell me: when was the last time you had a drink in an utterly sordid and disreputable tavern?"

Tregan grinned. "Not since I was a wild young troublemaker myself."

"Then I'll stand you one before we go back to Keenspur House."

*

Later, it was my turn to don a disguise. Clad in homespun with dirt beneath my nails, I became a prosperous but unsophisticated farmer from the Bronze River delta, dazzled by his first look at Balathex and eager for tales of her notorious fencing academies, duels, and blood feuds. Eager enough to buy wine, spirits, and supper for any knowledgeable local willing to regale me.

As I expected, many of Dromis's students were willing; they were as given to spendthrift habits as the other young rakes of my acquaintance, and thus often out of funds even when their families were wealthy. And once I had them talking and—I hoped—drunk enough to be indiscreet, I steered the conversation to their maestro.

It turned out that before coming to Balathex, he'd been a soldier in the High Hills, forced to flee after he killed a noble in a duel over a courtesan. Or a slaver in Chontemay, a bandit in Stone Angels, or a zealot who wound up on the losing side in a religious war fought somewhere far to the south. It depended on who was telling the story, or, for all I knew, they could all have been true. It didn't matter. There was nothing in any of them to account for his students' extraordinary string of victories.

Nor was their description of their training any more illuminating. Dromis seemed to teach pretty much the same techniques and principles as his rivals. When a student was about to fight a duel, he worked with him intensively, but the rest of us did that, too. If he used magic to enhance the efficacy of his instruction, his pupils didn't appear to know about it.

In the end, I decided I'd wasted both my money and my time, but I told myself it didn't matter. I'd find a way to unmask Dromis's perfidy eventually.

I didn't realize I was running out of time.

*

The Silver Trumpet was just downstairs from my own fencing academy, and it served the best trout, perch, and crawfish dishes in Balathex. I ate there often, so I don't suppose it was difficult for Dromis to find me there.

I didn't know he'd come in until the room fell silent, and Marissa, my companion at my corner table, turned in the direction of the door. "Damn it!" she snarled.

I looked where she was looking. Sneering, Dromis was stalking toward me with half a dozen of his students and Olissimal following after. The cripple smirked.

I realized I'd made an error consulting him; I'd underestimated his capacity for holding a grudge. I'd hoped that by allowing him into my school, I could win back what passed for his good will, and in fact, he had answered my questions. But then he'd plainly hurried to Dromis to tell him I was making inquiries into his affairs.

"Get up and draw!" Marissa said. I'd explained to her how Dromis's protégés preferred a formal duel to an impromptu fight. Accordingly, she surmised that I'd be better off in the latter, and I suspected the same.

Still, I didn't move.

"Do it!" she urged. "Lords Pivor and Baltes are your friends! They'll keep you out of trouble with the law!"

Possibly they would. But several of my pupils were in the room. If I drew, so would they, so too would Dromis's followers, and the gods only knew who or how many would die in the chaotic melee that would follow.

And even if I could prevent such a fracas by commanding my students to keep their seats, I'd labored to teach them that combat was serious business, best avoided whenever possible. If I jumped up and hurled myself at Dromis like a starving wolf, seemingly without provocation, it would make a mockery of all my homilies and admonitions.

So I simply ate another bite of batter-fried perch and waited for the yellow-beard and his companions to reach my table.

Once he arrived, he didn't waste any time. Glowering down at me, he said, "Olissimal tells me you claim I teach my duelists to cheat."

I hadn't, not to the cripple, not in so many words. Olissimal had figured out what I suspected for himself. Still, I saw no reason to deny it. It wouldn't change what was about to happen. "That's right," I said.

Dromis's students glared and muttered.

"Then I say you're a liar." Dromis pulled a daffodil-colored leather gauntlet from his belt and slapped it down on the tabletop. I picked it up and that was that.

"Marissa will act for me," I said.

"And Olissimal for me," Dromis replied.

Olissimal's leer stretched wider. "I wouldn't miss it for the world."

*

Later on, it occurred to me that perhaps I should be glad Dromis had challenged me. It gave me what I wanted: a chance to avenge Falnac's death.

For after all, I was reasonably confident of my own prowess. I'd survived three decades of warfare and duels. I'd destroyed a fire elemental, and the undead warlock in the vaults under Keenspur House. It was conceivable that I could defeat Dromis, too, no matter what tricks he had in store.

But I didn't really believe it. My instincts warned me I was in desperate trouble, and the only honorable way out was to uncover Dromis's secret.

Of course, not everyone would agree that housebreaking was "honorable," but given the circumstances, I was willing to make allowances.

Skulking in the same dark, narrow space where Tregan had performed his divination, I watched Dromis's school until all the lights went out, and for a while thereafter. Then I tied on my mask and, hooded lantern in hand, scurried across the benighted street and around to the back of the building, where there was a secondary entrance.

I didn't know how to pick a lock—I kept meaning to learn— but I did know how to break open a door with a crowbar. I waited until I was certain no one had heard the crunching noise it made, then crept into what proved to be a kitchen.

Shining my light only when absolutely necessary and only for an instant at a time, seeking the way to the top floor, I groped through darkness. In time, I passed bedchambers and heard the snoring buzzing from within, and I'll admit, it crossed my mind that I could settle this whole affair by killing Dromis in his sleep. But that would have made me just as vile as he was, especially considering that, my suspicions notwithstanding, I didn't yet have any proof that he and his pupils were cheats.

I pulled a folding staircase down from a ceiling to reach the garret. Once there, I risked letting my lantern shine continuously. As I played the beam about, it illuminated cobwebs, dusty trunks and crates, and then something more interesting.

It was a block of dark, silver-flecked stone, about the size of a horse's head, sitting on a table with a chair in front of it. Though I'd traveled far before settling in Balathex, I didn't recognize the type of mineral, nor the style of the glyphs carved into it, either. I certainly couldn't hazard a guess as to their meaning.

What I could tell was that the block was broken, some of the sigils, marred or defaced. Either the artifact had fallen from a height, or someone had taken a hammer to it. And, I could sense the power emanating from it, like a hum so faint that a man didn't quite realize he was hearing it.

Plainly, it was the talisman whose presence Tregan had discerned, and if he were here, playing burglar along with me, perhaps he could have told me what the magic did. In his absence, I'd have to try to discover on my own.

I sat down in the chair and inspected the block at close range. It didn't look appreciably different, nor did it react to my proximity. Warily, like a man testing the edge of a blade, I touched a fingertip to the front of it.

That one light contact was all it took. Suddenly everything vanished, including my sense of my own body. In its place there suddenly rushed a howling torrent of darkness that tumbled me along like a raging river. Except, not exactly. But that's as close as I can come to describing the sensation.

Terrified, I reached out—not with the hands I could no longer feel, but with sheer willpower, I think—for something other than the black rapids. It worked; abruptly, the nature of my experience changed. I could still feel the current sweeping me along, but now I was more like a man floating precariously on the surface than one drowning in the depths.

As a result, I could see. Balathex lay far below me, as if I were a hawk floating on the wind, while the sky arched overhead.

But the sky wasn't behaving properly. It flickered from dark to light and back again in an instant, quick as the beat of a hummingbird's wing.

Then the trees dropped their leaves almost as quickly. Snow blanketed the earth, then melted away. Several new houses sprang up, the frames clothing themselves in solid walls like a man pulling up a pair of breeches.

Panicked and befuddled though I was, I had a vague idea what was happening. The dark stone had drawn my spirit from my body. That trick was common enough that even non-magical folk like me had heard of it. What was unusual was that in the process, it had also yanked me loose from my proper position in time. Now something—perhaps simply the inexorable momentum of time—was whisking me into the future.

I was afraid that if it carried me too far, it would prove impossible to get back. I started swimming against the current, though my struggles had nothing to do with stroking arms or kicking legs. As before, it was a matter of pure resolve.

For a while, I couldn't tell if I was making any headway. Then, for just an instant, I caught a glimpse of the room and moment from which I'd come.

Unfortunately, my body wasn't alone anymore. Dromis was creeping up behind me with a dagger in his hand.

I struggled even harder, if that was possible, and fought the pressure until I was certain the effort had taken too long. If I managed to return to my body at all, it would be to find my life gushing from a slit throat.

But evidently a man's sense of time doesn't count for much when he's already come unstuck from it as it's commonly experienced. For suddenly I had a solid form again, and it seemed unwounded. I sensed Dromis looming just behind me.

I threw myself sideways out of the chair before he could cut me. He came after me, and, sprawled on my back, I kicked at him. I connected with his shin and knocked him staggering off balance.

That gave me time to roll to my feet and draw my sword. The trouble was that when I did, the floor seemed to pitch and I nearly fell down again. My forced jaunt into tomorrow had left me weak and dizzy. I couldn't win a fight with a fellow fencing master in this condition.

I bolted down the folding stairs. Dromis took a moment to unsheathe his own sword, then gave chase.

Given a chance, he'd catch me, too. He wasn't suffering from vertigo, and he was thoroughly familiar with the layout of the lightless house.

I spied a square of lesser darkness: a window on the far side of a doorway. I charged it and crashed through the laths and oiled paper.

I fell two stories and landed hard, but when I tried to stand up again, I could. I hadn't broken anything. Apparently unwilling to trust to fool's luck as I had, Dromis didn't jump after me. I staggered away into the night as fast as I was able.

*

Fortunately, the weakness and dizziness didn't last long. They were gone by the time Dromis came to call at my school the next morning.

As before, he appeared with several of his students tagging along, serving as bodyguards whether they realized it or not. But he consented to leave them loitering in the main training hall while he and I sat at a table in one of the alcoves along the wall. His disciples would still see it if I attempted any violence, and he likely realized I wouldn't talk honestly about breaking into his house if anyone else was close enough to overhear.

"How's your leg?" I asked him.

"Fine. You didn't kick me that hard." He took a breath. "I moved the stone. The City Guards can search my academy from top to bottom. They won't find a thing."

I shrugged. "Even if they did, I couldn't prove that the thing can be used to cheat at dueling, let alone that you actually have used it that way. Even though I'm sure of it."

He frowned. "What exactly is it that you think you know?"

"The talisman carries a man's spirit—and his perceptions—into the future. I couldn't control exactly where I went or what I saw. But you can, either because you know the words of command or just because you've practiced. Prior to a duel, you observe exactly how a student's opponent will behave, and precisely what the pupil does to overcome those tactics. Then you drill your fencer in the proper moves, and everything works out just as you foresaw. Magic gives him an unfair advantage even though no enchantments or banes are active on the field of honor.

"The only limitation," I continued, "is that to guarantee victory, you have to provide special instruction for each individual combat. But you've minimized that problem by stressing to your charges that formal duels are always to be preferred over impromptu bloodletting."

Dromis scowled. "I truly am a fine swordsman, and a fine teacher, too."

"If you say so."

"But since I had an edge, why not use it? How else could I achieve preeminence quickly in a city already famous for its fencing masters? You'd have done the same thing in my place."

I shook my head. "I'd use your stone or any other trick in war, but never in dueling. The code of the duel is an attempt to bring order and restraint to that which would otherwise be chaotic and bestial, and for that reason, civilized men value it."

He sneered. "I've always heard that Selden is a strong man, but you think like a weak one."

"Let's not debate moral philosophy. We're not likely to reach an accord. I'm much rather hear how you came by the stone."

"All right, why not, if you're curious. When I was as young as those lads"—he nodded toward his students—"a new creed arose in my homeland. Given the chance to flourish, it could have changed the world. But corrupt lords and false priests declared our prophet a demon in disguise, and hundreds of idiots believed them. An army marched on us when we were still too few to defend ourselves."

I remembered the stories his pupils told. "Then you really did fight on the losing side in a religious war."

He glared as if my matter-of-fact way of speaking was an insult to the exaltation and tragedy enshrined in his memory. "I survived the final battle, then returned to the temple of the prophet. The unbelievers had defaced the black stone along with everything else, but it was still a holy relic, and something about it called to me. I decided to carry it with me into exile, and when I touched it, it revealed its power to me."

"And you've no doubt cheated your way through life ever since."

"I'm tired of hearing you use that word. It's good to know that after we meet two mornings hence, I won't have to hear it anymore."

"Indeed not. You won't hear anything ever again."

Dromis laughed. "I thought you understood, Selden. You can't win. I've already watched our duel. I already know the tactics you'll employ even if you haven't yet decided on them yourself, and I know how I'll defeat them and cut you down. In a very real sense, you're already lying dead at my feet."

*

I found Marissa in her armory repairing a leather-and-wire-mesh fencing helmet. As she got caught up in my story, she abandoned her task, and left the protective mask to lie in pieces on the cluttered worktable before her.

"I told you we should kill Dromis before the duel," she said. "Luckily, it's not too late."

"Actually, it is," I replied. "He's hiding behind a wall of his students, and he'll stay there until he comes to keep our appointment."

"In that case, go to Lords Baltes and Pivor."

"Without proof?"

"You shouldn't need it. They owe you. They're your friends."

"They're also committed to governing the city in a less arbitrary manner than their predecessors, and that's a good thing. I won't ask them to set aside their own rules of law just to save my arse."

"Then what? You can't simply refuse to fight, or people will think you a coward. No maestro or mercenary can afford that."

I felt a jab of anger. "Don't worry about that. Despite everything, I want to duel. I want to beat Dromis at his own rotten game and pay him back for Falnac's death." I took a breath. "And even if I didn't, the dastard has evidently seen that I show up, so perhaps I don't have a choice. Maybe, somehow, I'd wind up at the designated place and time no matter what."

Marissa made a sour face. "That's so contrary to common sense, it makes my head hurt just to think about it."

"Mine too. So why don't we try thinking like warriors?"

*

A dank mist blurred the mausoleums and grave markers, and the dawn was just a luminous smear on a wall of gray cloud. The birds hadn't yet begun to sing.

I'd done my best to keep Dromis's prophecy of doom from affecting my morale. But perhaps the dismal morning helped to dampen my spirits, for as we approached one another, I did indeed have the fey sense that my fate was sealed. That all that was about to happen had, in some ultimate sense, happened already.

I couldn't afford to feel like a helpless sleepwalker, so I focused on Dromis's sneer and Olissimal's gloating smirk, stoking my hatred for them both. It wasn't something I would have done ordinarily; I prefer to fight with a cool head. But in this instance, it steadied me.

We took our places, and then Olissimal said, "We, your friends, urge you to seek a peaceful resolution to your dispute." I doubted that anyone in the history of swordplay had ever made that traditional plea with such a transparent lack of sincerity.

"I do not apologize," Dromis said, "and I know for a fact that my opponent won't, either. Isn't that right, Selden?" He grinned at me as though sharing a secret jest.

"Yes," I said.

"I'll always wonder: Could you simply not accept the truth of your situation, or did your notions of honor oblige you to show up even so? Either way, you'll die a fool."

I looked to Marissa. "Let's get on with it."

"As you wish," she said, backing away to give Dromis and me room to fight. Shifting his crutches, Olissimal likewise hobbled clear.

Marissa then lifted a white cloth and whipped it through the air. Dromis and I started to circle one another.

Fear welled up inside me, and of course, given the life I'd led, it was scarcely the first time. But it was the first time it balked me. For a heartbeat, I couldn't attack because the craven part of me knew that whatever technique I attempted, Dromis would offer a perfect—and perfectly lethal—response.

I screamed a battle cry to jolt myself into motion.

I sprang into the distance, feinted to the chest, and cut to the head. Dromis ducked under the stroke and thrust at my chest as he'd surely watched himself do while using the power of the stone.

It was a nasty counterattack, but fortunately, I was ready for it. I deflected it with a heavy beat-parry that weakened his grip on his hilt, then slashed at his face.

Dromis had boasted he was a good swordsman, and it was so. He didn't drop his weapon, and he managed to jump back and evade my cut. But his eyes were wide with shock. Whereas I wanted to laugh, because from this moment forward, nothing about our encounter was predestined. Now it was just another sword fight.

Having experienced the turbulent power of the stone, I'd conjectured that, while Dromis had learned to use it, the process wasn't easy for him. For after all, he was a warrior, not a mystic, and moreover, the artifact was damaged.

And if Dromis had to struggle mightily to swim through the time currents in the same way I had, then it stood to reason that he couldn't navigate to a scene he wanted to witness with any extraordinary precision. He had to flounder about until he happened across it, then fight to hold his position long enough to obtain a serviceable glimpse.

So I'd called in the favor owed me by the players of the Azure Swan Theater. On the previous morning, they, Marissa, and I had thrice staged a mock duel, with actors made up to resemble Dromis, a band of his students, and Olissimal. Each time I attacked with a feint to the chest and a cut to the head, and each time my adversary dispatched me with a stab to the torso. His sword was blunt, but still capable of breaking the bladder of pig's blood concealed inside my doublet.

The idea was for Dromis's spirit, adrift in time, to observe one of the fraudulent duels and mistake it for the real one, and I admit, I've hatched schemes that inspired greater confidence. Even if all my unsubstantiated guesses were correct, there was still one chance in four that my foe had watched the actual combat. But now I knew the trick had worked.

We traded attacks, neither scoring as of yet. But as the moments passed, I felt more and more in control of the action, and he had to give ground repeatedly.

I judged that if I could stop him retreating, I could finish him, and there was a marble tomb, crowned with a statue of a dove lighting on the hand of a goddess, several paces behind him. I started the process of backing him up against it.

Then Dromis used the thumb of his off hand to rotate the gold ring on his middle finger, perhaps another keepsake he'd carried away from his cult's desecrated temple. The medallion I wore next to my skin turned icy cold, warning me of hostile magic. Unfortunately, the warning was redundant. I was able to guess that my opponent had cast a curse stored in a talisman from the way the world suddenly went black.

Acting by reflex, I parried, and steel rang as I stopped Dromis's sword. I riposted, and felt my blade cleave flesh and stick there. When Dromis fell, his weight dragged it toward the ground.

My feat was lucky, but not, I think, pure luck. Throughout the duel, I'd studied Dromis's fighting style and learned his favorite attack. Thus, even blind, I was able to defend. And when our blades met, it gave me a sense of his position. That made it possible to land a cut.

Much to my relief, my eyesight returned to me a moment after Dromis dropped. Blinking away a certain residual cloudiness, I checked to make sure he was dead, then pivoted to find Olissimal. I wanted to witness his dismay at his champion's demise.

But in that regard, I was disappointed. Supported by his crutches, Olissimal stood shivering with his eyes half closed, a picture of perverse delight. He didn't really care who'd died a bloody death, only that someone had.

I suppose no moment is perfect. But, Olissimal's bliss notwithstanding, this one came close, and tasted sweeter still when Marissa strode up to me, a rare smile of genuine admiration on her face. "Nicely done," she said.

"You have no idea," I answered.

"So what happens now? We find the stone and try to use it to prove Dromis's duelists cheated?"

"No, because they didn't. Not knowingly. They didn't understand Dromis used sorcery to determine how they should fight. They just thought he was a brilliant teacher."

"Then we're done. I mean, except for collecting the stone and using it to pick winning horses."

I was reasonably certain she was joking. But since coming to Balathex, I'd lost a ridiculous amount of coin wagering in the hippodrome, and I confess that, just for an instant, I was tempted.

Light and Dark

When I left Balathex at the end of winter, to help a dying friend, Tregan Keenspur had been a robust and vigorous man. Now, with the spring rain drumming on the roof of his family mansion, he looked not just lean but gaunt and hobbled with the aid of an ebony cane. And when sudden pain made him suck in a hissing breath, I had to ask: "Are you sure you're up to this?"

He scowled. Wizards don't appreciate having their abilities questioned, nor do the nobly born, and he was both.

"It won't help anyone," I said, "if your heart gives out when you try to cast the spell."

"I still have strength enough," he replied. "Do you remember everything I told you? Do you know what to do with the club?"

"Yes."

"Then stand in front of the mirror."

Knowing what I knew, I did so with a certain amount of reluctance, even though he'd told me the curse took a little time to work, and that was assuming our adversary had even bothered to set a snare for me. The mirror was an oval big as a tower shield, the frame, a silver serpent swallowing its own tail. No doubt it was magical, but nothing uncanny happened until Tregan came to stand behind me. I cast a reflection, but he didn't. Up close, he stank of unhealthy sweat. He whispered words that made me feel muddled and dizzy, then poked me in the back with a soft touch. But the charge of power it carried sent me hurtling toward the glass.

Or at least that was how it felt. But when I threw up my arms to protect my face, flailing with the length of polished blue-green wood he'd given me, I found I was standing as steady and motionless as before. Only now I was facing away from the mirror, and Tregan was nowhere to be found. Thinking I might see him peering out of the glass, I looked around, but he wasn't there, either.

Tregan hadn't been able to supply a full explanation of what to expect in the mirror world, but he had warned me it might be strange and disorienting. On first inspection, it wasn't. I still appeared to be inside the mage's garret workroom with its stuffed harpy, racks of ritual staves and blades, and hint of incense hanging in the air. The only difference was that I didn't hear the rain on the roof anymore.

Still, it seemed a good idea to take my bearings. I moved to one of the windows, opened the shutters, then cursed in surprise.

In a way, it was still Balathex outside. I recognized landmarks, like the Temple of Regrets and—to my relief—the watchtower. Three of the many fountains that inspired poets to call my adopted home the Glittering City or the Whispering City were visible. But the city walls were missing, and in general, it was as if a demented god had shattered the place into pieces, discarded some, and reassembled the rest into a chaotic jumble. Some buildings had portions sliced away, exposing their interiors. A bathhouse had fused with a tannery that by rights should have stood on the opposite side of town. A length of street slanted up to the top of a house like a ramp.

The scene wasn't wholly bright. Though portions were, many weren't. But nothing seemed entirely dark, either. It all had a glossiness to it that muddled my sense of depth. At certain moments, the vista looked flat, like a landscape by a painter who hadn't mastered perspective. At others, it gave the impression of a hundred flat surfaces in juxtaposition, somewhat like the facets of a jewel.

And it all looked bright in contrast to the murk bordering it. Pools of blackness lurked wherever the various pieces fitted together imperfectly, and the town as a whole was an islet of light and form in an ocean of night.

In its essentials, it was as Tregan had said it would be. This Balathex was made of reflections of the original our enemy had harvested from one mirror or another. If an object or space hadn't cast its image somewhere, he couldn't include it. While the darkness was the preexisting otherworld—some empty precinct of the Lower Worlds, perhaps—in which he'd constructed his refuge.

Since nothing was where it ought to be, I wondered how much trouble I'd have finding my way around. Then I heard motion at my back.

I turned to see Tregan, who raised the sword in his hand. The blade moaned as he swung it at my head.

*

Balathex attracts a fair number of supernatural threats. And, more often than a sensible man would prefer, I find myself assigned the task of removing them. It's what I get for setting up shop as a special sort of mercenary, one who no longer marches off to war but claims to know how to handle smaller and sometimes stranger conflicts.

Despite that, when a wizard named Alexos Dambrin started practicing proscribed magic, I only played a small part in apprehending him. And when, weary and sore from my travels, I swung myself off my horse, I hadn't thought of him in months.

I tossed an iron penny to a boy who would take the animal back to the livery stable. Then I headed up the stairs to my rooms, which occupied the space above a tavern called the Goblin's Bloody Nose.

Just as I gripped the door handle, footsteps thudded behind me. I pivoted. A pudgy youth in the livery of the Keenspurs was scurrying up the steps. "Master Selden!" he gasped. "Don't go in there!"

"Why not?" I replied.

"Lord Tregan says please, " he said, still panting, "you have to come see him before you do anything else. He ordered me to watch for you. But I had to go into the alley to piss."

I would have liked to clean myself up and throw back a cup of wine, but if Tregan wanted to see me without delay, so be it. He and I were friends, to the extent that the difference in our social stations allowed.

So the servant and I hurried off to Keenspur House with its gables and eight-sided turrets. And when the plump lad led me into Tregan's presence, I was shocked at the gray, red-eyed appearance of his sharp-featured face.

"You're ill," I said.

"Not exactly," he said, and waved a tremulous hand to dismiss the lackey. He waited for the door to shut before continuing. "I'm cursed."

"Do you know who did it?" And when he named the name, I said, "I thought the tribunal hanged him."

He sighed. "Masters of black magic don't always die as easily as other men."

True enough, as my own experience attested.

"You'll recall," Tregan continued, "when Alexos started studying forbidden arts, his patron demons taught him to play tricks with mirrors."

I nodded. "He could peer into his own glass and see out of someone else's. He used what he discovered for blackmail."

"Yes. But it turns out he learned to do a lot more than that, and somehow, he must have gotten his hands on a mirror while he was awaiting execution. Because he escaped into it. The thing we sent to the gallows was only a kind of decoy."

"'Escaped into it' and came out where?"

He made a sour face. "Nowhere. Let me tell the story, and then you'll understand. After the hanging, we nobles began to fall ill. The sickness spread so quickly that it afflicted dozens of us before anyone noticed that we no longer cast reflections."

"Alexos stole them," I guessed. "And pieces of your souls, or your vitality, with them."

"Yes. The wretch gave us some time to worry, and then a message appeared inside certain mirrors. He demands a pardon, money, land, and marriage to a lady from one of the most prominent houses. Otherwise, he'll keep what he took and let us waste away."

"As ransoms go, it could be worse."

Tregan grimaced. "So far, I've managed to convince my peers that you don't capitulate to a practitioner of the proscribed arts. Aside from the dishonor, if you give in to such a blackguard today, there's no telling what new concessions he'll demand or what new atrocities he'll perpetrate tomorrow. It's much, much better to defeat him."

"In principle, I agree. And I take it that's where I come in."

"Yes. Once I knew we were dealing with Alexos, I set about trying to locate him. I discovered that he's created a sort of fortress for himself on the other side of the mirrors he used to curse us. I believe that, even weak as I am, I can send an agent there. Knowing you were due back soon, I thought of you."

"And stationed a man to catch me before I walked into my rooms and looked in the mirror on the wall. Just on the off chance that Alexos is laying for me, too."

"It's possible. You have a certain reputation."

I smiled. "I suppose I do. Still, in this situation, why wait for me, and why rely on me alone? Why not send a whole company of soldiers?"

"I told you, I'm weak. I don't know that I can send more than one man, and he needs to be someone discreet. Balathex has other enemies besides Alexos. Do you know what might happen if word got out that all the city fathers are ill?"

"I see your point."

"Then will you help?"

"If you can tell me how to break the curse."

We discussed the options, then my fee, and then he sent me through.

*

The real Tregan had become feeble and slow, but his counterpart hadn't. I hopped back barely in time to avoid the sword cut. The groan of the enchanted blade spiked to a screech as it missed my face by a finger length.

My first impulse was to drop the club and snatch for the broadsword at my side. But I feared doing mortal harm to the piece of my friend Alexos had stolen. So, gripping it with both hands, I hefted the length of wood into a middle guard. It was sturdy and well balanced, as long as an axe handle and slightly curved like one as well.

Mirror Tregan lifted the groaning sword as though for another head cut. I could see it was a feint, and parried the true attack when it flashed at my ribs.

I riposted with a blow to the shoulder. Bone crunched, and my opponent's sword arm flopped down limp at his side. His blade squirmed from his fingers and floated toward his off hand. I batted it across the room, then hit Tregan over the head. His legs buckled and spilled him to the floor.

I half expected his sword to fly up into the air and attack on its own, but it didn't. After a moment, it even stopped twitching and moaning.

When I was satisfied that it had no more tricks to play, I checked to make sure Tregan was still breathing. He was. Assuming I got his two halves reunited, he might have a sore head or even a broken shoulder, but nothing worse.

I started downstairs and encountered another disorienting surprise. The steps only went down a little way. The descent ended abruptly in a lady's bedchamber smelling of flowery perfume and full of wigs on head-shaped wooden stands.

The room wasn't where it should have been, but at least it belonged in the mansion somewhere. The space beyond the doorway didn't. It was a piece of the outdoors, a wedge of plaza with sunlight gleaming on freshly fallen snow. Icicles dripped from the rim of the big stone bowl in the center. My breath steamed as I hurried across.

With everything so thoroughly scrambled, it took a while just to find a way out of the mansion. Which wasn't all bad. It gave me time to decide on my next move.

I'd entered the mirror world thinking I'd probably attack and kill Alexos. According to Tregan, that should break the curse, and send everyone's reflection back where it belonged. And while I assumed it might be difficult, I'd defeated wizards before.

But now I knew Alexos hadn't just stolen the aristocrats' reflections. He'd turned them into slaves. Some, like Tregan's, were evidently playing watchdog at the entry points to his redoubt. But he might well be keeping others close to guard his person. And while fighting a single opponent is feasible, even if he is a warlock, taking on six or twelve is a more difficult proposition.

I also realized it was going to be challenging just to find my way around, and thus, quite possibly difficult even to locate Alexos. Whereas, once I groped my way out of Keenspur House, I should be able to see my alternate objective looming over everything else, and steer a course for it.

So I'd try the tactic Tregan had suggested.

Outside the mansion, in the gardens, I found the reflection of a relatively warm day, with no snow on the ground. I noticed again how everything but me possessed a subtle sheen. And how the light seemed to come from everywhere and nowhere, so that nothing cast a shadow.

Once I left Keenspur House behind, I occasionally spotted figures prowling in the distance. I hoped that if they saw me, too, they mistook me for one of their own.

Then I peeked around a corner and saw someone who wasn't distant. His silk and velvet garments a medley of blues, their foppish frills an odd contrast to his coarse features and burly frame, a lord named Grelldac was tramping in my direction. He was only a few paces away, and would surely have seen me, too, except that his head was turned at that particular moment.

Grelldac was one of Balathex's better duelists, and I wouldn't have been wildly enthusiastic about fighting him in the best of circumstances. I resolved to avoid his notice instead.

I snatched my head back and cast about. One of the partial houses, with its front wall missing, caught my eye. The interior was comparatively dim, and if I hid there, I had a fair chance of escaping detection.

Trying to move quietly, I scurried in that direction. My course took me near what looked like an utterly dark rift in the ground, one of the gaps between the ill-assembled puzzle pieces of Alexos's mad little world.

Suddenly I felt something glaring at me. My head throbbed, my guts churned, and I stumbled. If you've ever had a witch give you the evil eye, it was like that, malice so fierce it stabbed like a dagger.

Previously, I'd conjectured that Alexos had situated his stronghold in an empty precinct of the Lower Worlds. Evidently I'd been wrong about the empty part. There were creatures lurking in that limitless dark, and they didn't like intruders.

It was a somewhat disturbing revelation, but I didn't have time to dwell on it. I hurried on, took a deep breath, and the sick feeling faded. I crouched behind a table and chairs in the sundered house and watched Grelldac pass obliviously by.

Afterward, I did my best to stay away from both Alexos's wandering minions and the murky gaps, and reached the foot of the watchtower without further incident. Congratulating myself on making it that far, I pulled open the door, and my momentary feeling of accomplishment died abruptly.

The tower was here because a mirror, or at any rate, some reflective surface, had captured the image of the exterior. But nothing had ever reflected the interior, or if it had, Alexos hadn't incorporated that particular semblance into his creation. And so there were no stairs, just a pocket of absolute darkness, and the feeling of hostile eyes peering out.

Inconvenient, but I wasn't beaten yet. I was no master climber, but as a soldier, I'd learned how to go up a wall. I just had to find rope, and something to serve as a grappling hook.

I'm not sure how long it took. It was hard to judge the passage of time without a sun or moon arcing across the sky. But eventually I had what I needed. First I climbed to the roof of a house that Alexos's magic had planted next to the watchtower, then scaled the taller structure.

That last part was nerve-wracking. It seemed likely that Alexos or one of his slaves would glance up at the skyline and see me. But I swung myself into the belfry without anyone raising the alarm.

Fortunately, the inside of the top of the tower was in existence, although I still saw nothing but blackness in the shaft beneath. I pulled the club from my belt and stood in front of the huge bronze bell.

Tregan had based his scheme on the notion that a realm created from mirrors would in some mystical sense share their properties. And on the truth that sound can shatter glass.

He was also counting on the fact that the ancient bell, forged to warn of fire, raiders, or dangerous beasts emerging from the Forest of Thorns, bore certain enchantments. If I rang that magical artifact by beating it with my similarly enchanted stick, it should raise a vibration that would demolish Alexos's artificial world.

At first I couldn't tell if my efforts were doing anything useful, only that the resulting clangor was painfully loud. But despite the discomfort and my concern for my hearing, I persevered. And gradually, the cityscape around me began to tremble.

But at the same time, the enslaved reflections scurried into view, all rushing toward the tower. They hadn't noticed me climbing it, but they and their master could hardly miss the pealing of the bell or the incipient earthquake. It was odd to see the august city fathers, as Tregan had called them, behaving like a mob, with me the object of their murderous intent.

Odd and alarming. Hoping to put an end to this affair before they reached the spire, I pounded the bell as hard and fast as I could.

Ripples ran through the city as they might across the surface of a pond, or through a piece of sheet metal when someone shakes it. But Alexos's Balathex stubbornly refused to shatter.

Hoping Tregan's plan simply needed more time to work, I stuck with it as long as I dared. But I couldn't let Alexos's servants surround the watchtower and trap me. So finally I slid back down the rope, hung by my hands from the eaves of the adjacent house, and dropped to the street below.

A shoulder roll kept me from breaking any bones, but as I scrambled to my feet, I saw that I might have waited too long to attempt my escape. A lord equipped with a hand-and-a-half sword and a frail-looking white-haired matriarch incongruously armed with a battle-axe were already close enough to pose a threat. They moved to flank me.

I lunged and swung my club at the lady's torso. She tried to catch the stroke on her axe, but reacted too slowly. The impact knocked her on her rump.

I spun around just as the noble swung his long, heavy sword in a horizontal arc. I ducked underneath it and stabbed the tip of my weapon into his groin at the same time. His mouth fell open, and he froze.

That gave me the chance to break away. And I needed to, because three more of Alexos's slaves were only a few strides away, with still more pounding up behind them.

I ran, sometimes dodging in and out of the split and tangled buildings in an effort to shake my pursuers off my track. It didn't work.

Perhaps it would have, except that the watchtower stood near the edge of the city, which limited my room to maneuver. And in time, the preeminent lords and ladies of the city herded me to a spot where light and shape gave way to murk. When I looked out at the darkness, I could feel depth, that space extended on and on in front of me, but I can't tell you how, because I certainly couldn't see that. Since the gloom was absolute, I might as well have been looking at a black wall. In fact, if I hadn't still had bits of the city at the edges of my vision when I peered at what lay beyond, I might have imagined I'd been struck blind.

There were at least twenty pursuers rapidly closing in on me. Even if I hadn't been winded, it would have been preposterous to imagine I could withstand them all. And then Alexos himself appeared behind them.

He was a small man with only a few wisps of mouse-colored hair left on the top of his head, who didn't look like the popular notion of an evil sorcerer. He didn't move in a swirl of black robes or laugh fiendishly, nor did a red light gleam in his eyes. But there was a sly, unwholesome avidity in his face. You wouldn't suspect him of casting the enchantments that brought a city to its knees, but you would have had no trouble imagining him peeping at lovers through a window.

He smirked at me and raised a small round mirror he held palmed in his left hand.

That final threat spurred me into motion. Frightened at the prospect but believing it my only chance, I whirled, ran into the dark, and discovered that being inside it didn't make whatever it hid any more visible. At that moment, it was like I truly was blind, and blundering through a place as chilly as a late autumn night.

I half expected to fall, but didn't. I still had solid ground beneath my feet, even if I couldn't see it anymore, or my feet, either.

I glanced back, and then, somewhat to my surprise, there was something to see. Glowing with their subtle inner light, the false Balathex and its inhabitants were still visible even though nothing else was. So I could tell that no one was pursuing me over the border.

But Alexos was chanting and sweeping the little mirror through serpentine passes. Perhaps he could still see me, even shrouded in the gloom.

I ran a zigzag course to throw off his aim. I didn't know if that would help, but I didn't know that it wouldn't, either.

The ground rose beneath me. The incline tripped me and nearly made me fall, but I caught my balance and dashed on. I passed over the crest of the rise and threw myself down on the other side, where I had cover.

Then I crawled over what felt like pebbles and weeds. When I raised my head and looked around again, the false Balathex was far enough away that it seemed reasonable to hope Alexos had lost track of me. Although he'd no doubt have guards patrolling the perimeter to catch me when I tried to sneak back in.

Maybe they wouldn't intercept me if I slipped all the way around to the opposite side. Was I willing to trek that far through the darkland? I decided I was, and then a spasm of nausea churned my guts.

I realized another devil had found me. I tossed the cudgel to my off hand and snatched for the hilt of my sword.

Cold hands gripped my forearm. Something hard bashed the back of my head. Stunned, I dropped to my knees. Tregan's club twisted out of my hand, and my sword and dagger whispered out of their sheaths. I belatedly comprehended that a whole pack of darklanders had accosted me.

Their hatred hammered me until I retched, and my head felt like an egg hatching an impatient chick. Finally they stopped giving me the evil eye. Then a couple of them grabbed me, hoisted me up, and held me from behind.

"Hurt him!" a darklander rasped. "Pick the soft things out of his face."

I still felt sick, but since I surmised the creature meant my eyes, that suggestion roused me. I stamped on feet and kicked backward into shins. Wrenched free of grasping fingers, lashed out with a punch, and connected. Since I was blind and outnumbered, I must have caught the darklanders by surprise to accomplish even that much. They hadn't imagined I had any fight left in me.

"Don't hurt me!" I gasped. "I'm not one of the invaders. I came to help you get rid of them." It was the only thing I could think of to say that had any hope at all of deterring them.

And it worked. They hesitated. Then one of them—I thought it was the same one who wanted to pluck my eyes out—said, "He's lying!"

"No," I said. "The city shines. Its people shine. But I don't."

"Now he's just babbling!" my ill wisher said. At which point I realized that creatures who evidently had no eyes were unlikely to know what glowed and what didn't.

But another darklander said, "I think he means the stink. The burning." This new voice snarled and scraped like the other, but was higher pitched, and I wondered if the speaker was female. "And it's true, it doesn't bleed from him like it does from the rest."

"But his shape!" said the first darklander. "His shape is exactly the same."

"Because I come from the same world," I said. "Alexos Dambrin—the sorcerer who built the city—is an outlaw, and I followed him here to kill him. When I do, it will break his power, and everything he created will disappear."

"It might," said a third darklander, with the most guttural voice yet, "but you can't kill the warlock and his guards. You ran from them. I watched."

"So kill him," said my ill wisher. "He may not sweat poison, but he's a trespasser like the rest."

"I admit," I said, "the first method I tried didn't work. But I could kill Alexos if I had allies to keep his servants off my back. If you want to get rid of him, then help me. Let's storm his fortress together."

A prolonged silence followed. Finally the female said, "We can't." Her voice still grated and set my teeth on edge, but even so, she sounded sheepish.

"Why not?" I asked.

"There's no trace of our realm left in the poison spaces," she said. "No way in, and nothing to sustain our lives if we did get in."

"You mean," I said, "there's no true darkness, and there needs to be."

"And so," snarled the first demon, "we have no use for you."

"Maybe you do," I said. "What if I can produce at least a little darkness, a bit of the conditions that are natural to you, inside the city? Will that help?"

"It might," the female said. "Open any breach, and my magic should be able to widen it."

"Then we have a chance. But you'll have to let me sneak back across the border."

My ill wisher laughed. "He just wants to escape where we can't follow."

"It wouldn't be much of an escape," I said, "since Alexos and his warriors want to kill me, too."

"I still don't like it," the creature said.

"Do you like it that several of our people are trapped inside that foul place?" the sorceress asked. "Or that it's a festering sore making the whole land sick? If the monster claims he can help us, I say, give him the chance. What do we have to lose?"

Other darklanders clamored in agreement. Eventually it became apparent that the majority favored helping me, which evidently meant they all would.

"If you're with me," I said, "there's one more thing you need to understand."

"What?" the sorceress asked.

"We should all try to kill Alexos," I said. "But you can't kill his servants. They're innocents enslaved by magic. You can subdue and restrain them, but nothing more."

"That isn't how we fight," the female said.

"It has to be this time around. Otherwise, I won't help you, your trapped friends will stay trapped, and your country will continue to rot."

Another silence, long enough for me to wonder if I'd spoiled the deal and so consigned myself to a painful death. Then: "All right. Your kind seem puny enough that we should be able to manage as you say."

"In that case, I recommend we go in through the opposite side of the city." As we made our way there, I likely amused my companions with my periodic stumbles.

Eventually we reached what looked like a good way in, since none of Alexos's sentries were in view. Someone placed my weapons in my hand, one at a time. Then somebody else gave me a nudge to start me walking.

I confess that for a moment, when I crossed back into the light, I felt tempted to forsake the darklanders. They were demons, after all, and who knew what might come of trusting them? But breaking our compact wouldn't put me any closer to thwarting Alexos.

So I turned back around toward the dark and positioned myself at the very edge of the false Balathex.

I'd noted the lack of shadows in the city. But, standing where I was, I had virtually all of its light behind me, and just a narrow section of its fading rim in front. I prayed that here, some hint of my shadow would appear, and it did. A faint gray streak connected my feet to the impenetrable murk less than a pace away.

"Is it enough?" I asked.

"Yes," said the female's voice from out of the gloom. "Back away slowly."

I did. I was worried the shadow would disappear, but it didn't. To the contrary. It darkened, and widened to cover a bigger patch of ground. When it was black and broad enough, the darklanders swarmed in.

I'd pictured them as we often picture devils, essentially human only uglier, with a bestial feature or two. Now I discovered they were considerably more peculiar. Gray-black in color, they trotted or skittered on round little feet and skinny legs like the limbs of horses. But the number of legs varied from three to as many as eight. The same was true of their arms, which might sprout from their torsos at any point, like branches from a tree trunk. In contrast to the jointed legs, the upper limbs writhed and coiled like snakes, and terminated in a diversity of appendages. Some were hands, others, serrated blades and hooks.

And, most strangely of all, the darklanders had no heads. Instead, clumps of growths like big leaves waved at the tops of their torsos. The individual leaves drooped, reared, and swiveled from one moment to the next. I guessed they were the demons' ears, and possibly other sensory organs as well.

"Ready?" asked the sorceress. Her voice sounded from the center of her sheaf of leaves.

I took a breath and shook off my astonishment and revulsion at the creatures' appearances. Well, enough to function, anyway. "Yes."

As we headed deeper into the city, I realized I didn't see my shadow splashed across the ground anymore. Rather, the darklanders and I advanced in a gloom like deep twilight. Sometimes, when it washed across one of the rifts between reflections, another demon would scuttle forth to join our band.

We found Alexos and a goodly number of his minions crossing a plaza near the center of town. Evidently he'd gotten tired of waiting for me to reappear at the border. Maybe he assumed that if I hadn't sneaked back into his domain already, the darklanders must have killed me.

He certainly hadn't expected me to ally with them, or find a way to lead them into his territory. His dangling jaw and goggling stare attested to that.

My companions and I charged.

Recovering from his shock, Alexos screamed for his slaves to defend him, and the nobles scrambled to obey. Inwardly I cringed, suddenly sure the darklanders would forget their promise and start killing. They didn't, though. They battered and grappled, but didn't slash or stab.

It cost them, too. The lords of Balathex had weapons and were proficient in their use. One demon fell, and then another, blood black as ink spurting from their wounds. But more of the time, it was they who, with their several limbs, pummeled or throttled an opponent until he couldn't fight anymore.

Trying to reach Alexos, I circled around knots of struggling combatants. Meanwhile, he brandished his mirror and shrilled words of power. Light blazed from the glass as though it reflected the sun.

It all but blinded me. Worse, it dispelled the gloom birthed from my shadow. Well, apparently not every trace of it, for the darklanders didn't drop dead instantly. But some of them screamed, and they all faltered. Taking advantage of their distress, Alexos's guards struck more of them down.

The sorceress croaked an incantation perhaps intended to keep the glare from burning the very last of the dark away. I finally reached a spot where I had a clear path to Alexos. I raised my arm to shield my eyes and rushed him.

Though nearly sightless—it was obviously my day for it—I glimpsed someone big driving in on the left. I pivoted and saw it was Grelldac. I used Tregan's club to beat aside his rapier thrust, then hit him four times, once in the knee and three times about the head. Afterward, he still clung to consciousness, but was incapable of bothering me for a while.

I dropped the stick, drew my broadsword, and dashed on.

Alexos may have done something overt with the mirror, like thrusting it in my direction, but if so, I couldn't see it. It was a change in the color of the light ahead, from dazzling white to yellow, that prompted me to dodge. Flame crackled past me.

I plunged into the distance, feinted to the chest, then cut at the place where, amid the glare, I judged Alexos's forearm to be. My aim was good. The sword sliced flesh, and the mirror tumbled from the warlock's hand. The blaze inside it died.

"Wait!" Alexos yelped. "The nobles are going to give in to me! They have to! I'll share everything with you!"

I lifted the sword for another attack.

Suddenly his one form multiplied into five, standing in a semicircle around me. Acting in perfect unison, they snapped the arms I hadn't wounded, and daggers flew out of their sleeves into their hands. They lunged at me, thrusting for my midsection.

Apparently Alexos thought the trick would so disconcert me that I'd lose track of which opponent was real, and which, illusory. I didn't. I stepped back and met the genuine mage with a stop thrust to the heart. He and the duplicates crumpled together, but the latter popped like soap bubbles before they reached the ground.

I looked around and saw that the reflections of the nobles were vanishing, too. The false Balathex started shaking. A tavern shattered into tiny fragments.

Struggling to keep my footing on the shuddering ground, I peered around for the sorceress. I think I found her, but it was difficult to tell one darklander from another. "Thank you!" I called.

"No, thank you!" she answered. "You've spilled mortal blood here, and with it, I can make a key to unlock the door of this prison."

"What do you mean? I thought you were happy in this—"

The whole city burst, and every bit of its light went out. I reeled through blackness for a dizzy moment, and then I was floundering about in Tregan's garret.

He looked stronger already, his color, better. But I still had to ask: "Is everything all right now?"

"I believe so." He grinned. "Except that it appears in addition to breaking my speculum, you've lost my wand."

I glanced around and saw that he was right about the mirror. It lay in pieces on the floor.

"And you?" Tregan asked. "Are you well? You have a strange expression on your face."

"There were demons on the other side of the glass. I had to make an alliance with them to deal with Alexos, and I may have helped them more than I meant to." I took a breath. "But to hell with it. With luck, that will end up being somebody else's problem."

The Silent Singer

I hadn't wanted to go to Kreelan's Plaint, not to listen to the bards and would-be bards of the southlands compete and not to keep the peace. I was busy running my fencing academy. "What are they going to do if they do get rowdy," I'd asked, "sing at one another?"

Apparently it could get more serious than that.

Pivor, half a dozen of his retainers, and I had just ridden into the town square, which was jammed with folk who'd come to enjoy the festival and vendors of beer, sausages, and trinkets eager to separate them from their coin. My aristocratically slim and elegantly attired patron was flying the Snow Lynx banner that identified him as the lord, albeit, mostly in absentia, of "the Plaint," but even so, the press was such that the commoners couldn't make way quickly even if they recognized him.

On the far side of the square, a redheaded woman backed out of a tavern's open door. Cloaked in gray, a soft cap sporting a pheasant feather on her head, she held a gnarled staff poised for defense.

An angry-looking man with a black snake embroidered on his jerkin followed her. The staff flicked out and clouted him on the temple.

He clutched his forehead and stumbled back with the fight knocked out of him. But two more men wearing the same emblem came through the doorway. When they saw what had befallen their fellow, they snatched for the daggers on their belts.

By then, I was already trying to push my horse through the crowd. But it was still slow going, and the appearance of sharp steel made the matter urgent.

Beside me was an elevated stage. I scrambled from the saddle onto the platform and sprinted across it.

Which didn't get me all the way up to the tavern. But beyond the stage was a row of vendors' stalls. Some had roofs. Others at least had uprights framing the counter with a signboard cross-piece connecting the top of one to the other. With a silent curse for my own recklessness, I sprang to the first.

Never intended to support a person's weight, the rickety temporary structures swayed and bounced, cracked and crunched, beneath me. But I kept moving, never obliging any one spot to hold me for more than an instant, and although I was no tumbler or ropewalker, I possessed a swordsman's sense of balance. That sufficed to see me safely to the last stall in line, from which I gratefully jumped to the ground.

The dagger men had spread out to flank the woman with the coppery hair. She shifted the staff back and forth in an effort to fend off both of them.

"Stop!" I bellowed. Startled, the three combatants looked in my direction. "I order you, and I'm Lord Pivor's agent!"

I was wearing the silver and ivory medallion he'd given me to prove it, too. But the nearer of the dagger men, a horse-faced fellow with a mustache in need of trimming, sneered and retorted, "And we're Lord Amseroth's men! Stay out of this, or we'll slice you, too!"

Under other circumstances, that would have made me draw my broadsword. But from the clench-fingered, inexpert way he gripped the knife, I was willing to gamble I could subdue him without it. I stepped in, inviting a stab, and when it came, I twisted aside and hit him in the jaw with the heel of my palm. That staggered him long enough for a kick in the knee. Bone cracked, and he cried out and fell.

Confident he was done, I glanced around just in time to see the redhead incapacitate the remaining black snake with a jab to the groin. As I winced in masculine sympathy, she shot me a grin. "Thanks!" she called.

"Don't thank me yet," I replied. "Not until I find out who started this."

"I can tell you that," said a voice from the doorway.

I turned. The speaker was a plump fellow who also wore the serpent badge, but embroidered on finer clothing. Like his chestnut hair bobbed at the bottom of the ears, the caffa doublet would have been in fashion in Balathex, where Pivor and I hailed from, a year or two previously.

The staff fighter started toward him.

"No!" I snapped.

With a scowl, she stopped short.

"That lunatic accused me of murder," said the pudgy man. "My friends took offense on my behalf."

"You are a murderer!" the woman said.

"If someone's been killed," I said, "the culprit will answer for it. But I need to hear the facts, starting with your names."

"I'm Dyllonna," said the woman. "A bard."

"A wandering bard," said the plump man, putting her in her place, not that the distinction meant much to me. I'd grown up far to the east, spent much of my adulthood as a traveling mercenary, and the citified nobles of Balathex didn't keep household bards anymore. They left that to their country cousins.

"And you?" I asked.

He raised an eyebrow as though surprised I didn't know. "Rogros. Bard to…well, you already heard which lord. Also, reigning champion in the ballad competition."

"Because you killed the better singer!" Dyllonna said.

"Hold on," I said. "I thought the contests hadn't started yet."

"At the last festival!" she said. Three years past.

"A robber slit Evdel's throat in an alley," Rogros said. "I had nothing to do with it."

Dyllonna glowered at me. "You said you'd make the murderer pay."

"When I said that, I assumed the death had just happened. I'd need some sort of evidence to look into it at this late date even if the enquiry fell within the scope of my duties."

Rogros smiled.

Dyllonna snarled, "You're afraid of crossing his master just like all the rest!"

"I'm working for Lord Pivor," I reiterated. "I'm not afraid—"

"Evdel will have justice." She turned and stalked away through the crowd, the nearer of whom had turned into gawking spectators.

"If that bitch keeps slandering me," Rogros said, "I'll expect you to deal with it."

"Collect your friends and go back inside," I said, "or you'll wish you had."

Something in my manner convinced him to heed me. As the last of his cronies limped back into the tavern, Pivor and his retinue rode up. The blond patrician was leading my abandoned mare.

"What was all that about?" he asked.

I swung myself back onto my steed. "I'll tell you on the way."

It wasn't a long story, but the house he kept here in town was only a block away. I had to suspend the telling while the butler, groom, maid, cook, and gardener lined up to welcome him, and I reflected that it must be soft work serving an employer who only turned up once a year.

I finished my account lounging in a leather chair with a glass of a tart white local vintage in hand, which certainly made the task more congenial. At the end, Pivor arched a barber-sculpted eyebrow. It was apparently my day for it.

"Are you going to look into it?" he asked.

"No. Why would I?"

"You're Selden. Solver of problems and mysteries."

"Only when being paid for it." I hesitated. "Am I? Obviously, if you want me to…"

He waved his hand, and the diamonds in his rings flashed in the sunlight shining through the window. "No, no. From our perspective, the festival isn't about the bards, murdered or otherwise. It's about backwater lords gathering to negotiate dowries, trade agreements, and ends to any feuds that have broken out since the last one. And as the master of Kreelan's Plaint, it's my responsibility to provide a peaceful, pleasant atmosphere for the dickering. Focus on that."

I did. With the aid, actual or hypothetical, of the men-at-arms Pivor put under my direction and the doddering old town constable, I collared cutpurses and cardsharps and averted brawls among hotheads who evidently felt that if their feuding families were going to make peace a day or two hence, they should make the most of the time they had left.

Through it all, though, Dyllonna's accusation stuck in my head. I found myself keeping a particular watch for her and Rogros when I wasn't busy with something else.

I spotted Dyllonna first. She was telling jokes and reciting comical poems on a corner with her cap upended on the ground to catch coins. With her wide mouth grinning and her green eyes shining, her freckled face looked prettier than it had twisted with hate.

Unfortunately, I put an end to that myself, by moving to toss a silver piece in the cap. When she noticed me, the scowl came back, and I reflected that you know you truly have offended a busker when she spurns your money.

Rogros had no need to pander to the vulgar mob. Instead, he made a point of greeting the seven "high bards" when their processional marched into town to judge the first competition of the children who aspired to study under their tutelage.

Bards, you see, occupied three rungs on a ladder. At the bottom were wandering entertainers like Dyllonna. Above them were the elite who'd secured positions in noble households, like Rogros. But at the very top were the masters who preserved the traditions, trained the next generation, and exercised authority over the craft. Their enclave was by a grove outside Kreelan's Plaint, which was why it fell to Pivor to oversee the festival.

The youngest of the high bards looked at least as old as me, and I've entered my middle years. A couple appeared as elderly as my new and mostly useless ally the constable. But by all accounts, the music of each and every one was magnificent, and since I was going to be stuck in town anyway, I'd hoped to hear one or more of them perform.

For now, though, I eavesdropped as Rogros complained about Dyllonna's accusations. The high bards appeared to take his grievance seriously, but in the end, couldn't agree on what to do about it. Frustrated, the plump singer strained to remain deferential as he took his leave of them.

I felt vaguely pleased despite the fact that it might make my life simpler if Dyllonna's superiors sent her packing. But even if she was wrong about Rogros, it didn't seem to me that she deserved it. Perhaps seeing three of his ruffian friends attack her had made me sympathetic.

But not sympathetic enough to tolerate her causing any more disturbances. I caught up with her again that night, when she was regaling a cellar tavern full of topers and whores with jests more ribald than the ones she'd told on the corner.

I made sure she didn't notice me, and then, covering a yawn with my hand, shadowed her when she gave over the stage to a lute player and headed out into the night. I hoped to see her to wherever she was sleeping and then seek my own bed.

Instead, she slipped into the mouth of a murky alleyway and started watching a frame house with corbelled upper stories and a tiled façade that stood cattycorner across the street.

I had no idea why. As a sign proclaimed, the potter who lived there was renting floor space to out-of-towners, but Rogros surely wasn't one of them. He'd stay with the rest of Amseroth's entourage in the inn called the Harp and Tambour.

I decided I needed to keep watching Dyllonna. I circled around the block, came up behind her, and found a hiding place several paces back.

As time crawled by, the bard shifted from foot to foot and occasionally gave a sigh. She was either impatient for something to happen or dissatisfied with her vantage point. Spying on some place or person, I'd sometimes felt the same.

Suddenly there came a bang, and then a confusion of voices. I realized someone had thrown the house's front door open, and now people were spilling out into the street. "The physician's on Duck Lane!" a woman shrilled.

Dyllonna ran toward the commotion. I ran after her.

When I caught up, she was staring into the pallid, wide-eyed face of the black-haired lass who was the object of everyone's concern. The latter had blood oozing from a nick on her throat. Had she been a man, I might have thought she'd nicked herself shaving.

"Tell me what happened!" Dyllonna said.

The stricken woman—looking at her, you could tell she was stricken somehow—gaped back like a simpleton.

"Was it Rogros?" the redhead persisted. "Was it?"

The afflicted lass's mouth worked, but no sound came out.

"If anyone did this," I said, "someone needs to find him." I dashed on toward the open door, and after a moment, Dyllonna's footsteps thumped after me.

Despite the dozen people who'd brought the stricken woman outdoors, the floors were still littered with snoring folk who'd either decided whatever was happening was none of their affair or never wakened to begin with. Picking my way among them, occasionally stepping or tripping on one in the dark, I stalked from room to room until I found a casement with the oiled-paper leaves open wide.

Since Dyllonna had been watching the front door, it was a reasonable assumption the malefactor had entered this way, although how he'd passed through without disturbing any of the sleepers was a puzzle. It was a fair bet that he'd already fled this way as well.

I jumped out the window into the street beyond and turned right. The Harp and Tambour lay in that direction. Dyllonna kept following and we hurried along together, peering in the hope of seeing some suspicious soul scurrying before us.

"You were watching me," she said, keeping her voice low.

"What matters," I replied, "is who the victim is and why you were watching her."

"At every festival," Dyllonna said, "there are bards everyone expects to excel. Many people believed Olette would win the ballad competition."

"So you were waiting for Rogros to try to kill her, to catch him in the act."

"Yes. But he was too cunning for me."

"We'll see about that."

A moment later, we heard uneven footsteps clumping along in the darkness ahead. Perhaps Rogros had turned his ankle jumping out the casement and now was limping.

Dyllonna and I sprinted forward. Then I felt twinges in my calf. When I looked down, a rat was clinging above the top of my boot, digging its claws through my breeches to hang on. Discomfort exploded into pain as it sank its chisel teeth into my leg.

I yanked the rodent free and crushed the squirming thing in my grip. By then, though, others were climbing my body. I snatched out my dagger and stabbed. Twice, I nearly put a hole in myself, but for the most part, I pierced the scrabbling, biting rodents instead.

Behind me, Dyllonna was no doubt engaged in a similar struggle, but she was also chanting.

A rat ran up my face. I closed my eye an instant before the animal's nails would otherwise have raked across it. Then it and all its fellows jumped off me and fled.

I turned. Dyllonna's small attackers were forsaking the fight as well, and though she was mottled with bloody bites and scratches like I was, she gave me a nod to signal that she could still function. We ran onward.

In fact, we ran the rest of the way to the coach gate of the Harp and Tambour, where glowing blue lanterns bracketed the entry. But we didn't catch up with our quarry.

Ignoring the porter, who seemed of the opinion that folk spotted with rat bites didn't belong in such a fine establishment, I threw open the tall azure door. Then Dyllonna and I followed the sounds of roistering.

They led me to a common room hung with black snake banners. A bushy-bearded, barrel-chested sort, the antithesis of Pivor and sophisticated patricians like him, Amseroth was boozing and playing quoits with his followers and friends, tossing the rings at the antlers of a stag head mounted on the wall. I'd pretty much expected such a scene. I hadn't expected Rogros to be there, too.

I started to warn Dyllonna to hold her tongue but was too slow. "Murderer!" she shouted.

Everyone turned to stare at us.

"Tonight," she continued, "you attacked Olette!"

Amseroth frowned. "Rogros has been here all night."

Dyllonna hesitated. That gave me time to elbow her in the ribs.

"Your pardon, my lord," I said. "Something unpleasant did happen just a short time ago, and Dyllonna was in the thick of it. She's understandably upset. But I see now it had nothing to do with your man, so we'll take our leave."

"I want her gone!" Rogros said. "Gone or locked up!"

"I understand," I said, meanwhile more or less manhandling Dyllonna out the door.

As I pulled it shut, she demanded, "How could you do that?"

"What," I replied, "haul you out of there before banishment or the town jail became unavoidable? Rogros isn't our man. Even if Amseroth was willing to lie for him, even if every other drunkard in the room had the presence of mind to uphold the deception, our well-fed friend wasn't out of breath, nor was he any more disheveled than an evening's revelry would explain."

She scowled. "Then it was one of his cronies."

"The three who tried to hurt you this afternoon were in the room as well, and if one of them had come rushing in moments before us, there would have been some sign of it. Somebody's eyes would have shifted in his direction when you were making your accusation."

"Well, that doesn't prove Rogros didn't kill Evdel!"

"Not conclusively, but it suggests he didn't."

"He hated Evdel!"

"If my assessment of Rogros's character is correct, he hates everyone who sings better than he does. Let's find the physician who's tending Olette. With luck, she's recovered from the shock and can tell us what happened. Besides, we could do with some tending ourselves."

"All right."

As we tramped along, I said, "I take it that you and Evdel were close."

It took her a couple steps to frame her answer. Then: "I don't sing all that well. I barely passed my examinations. Evdel could have kept company with bards as gifted as himself, or fancy ladies. But whenever our paths crossed, he chose me."

"I like a good joke as much as a good tune."

"So do I. But the heart of the bardic arts is music, which means..." She shook her head, and her wavy hair swished on the collar of her stained old traveler's cloak. "It means I've spent the past three years brooding over Evdel's murder, and when Rogros and I came together again, I felt I had to do something about it. Now..."

"Now," I said, "we'll see what we can discover."

The physician was a scrawny fellow with side-whiskers and a needle nose. He didn't like being called away from his patient, but the sight of my badge of authority mollified him. Or maybe it was the realization that Dyllonna and I were likewise in need of care.

"See to my friend first," I said, "and while you're about it, tell me about Olette. Is she ready to answer questions?"

"No," the doctor said, "nor is she likely to become so."

"Why not?"

"It will make more sense if I show you." He then faltered as if realizing he couldn't do that and dab at Dyllonna's cheek with a swab at the same time.

"I'll keep." The bard gestured to the door the physician had just come through. "Olette's this way?"

She was, and she cowered as we entered. But the physician spoke to her gently, and, trembling, she allowed him to tug on her chin and open her mouth.

Her tongue was gray and withered. So were the gums and the rest of the tissue I could see. Dyllonna gasped.

"Acid?" I asked. "Or something hot?"

"If it had been," the physician said, "she'd be in pain, and that doesn't appear to be the case."

"Olette," I said, "can you write?"

She didn't seem to register that I was talking to her.

I turned back to the physician. "How long before she returns to her senses?"

He shook his head. "So far, there's no indication that she will. We don't know that only the mouth is shriveled. It's possible the brain is compromised as well."

I bit back an obscenity.

Dyllonna and I departed the premises greasy with salve and mottled with sticking plasters. I then cast about for somewhere to buy a drink. Fortunately, with the festival in full swing, a vendor's stall was easy to find.

When I finished my brandy and returned the clay goblet, I said, "So, magic."

Dyllonna wiped beer foam from her lips. "You're sure?"

"I had my suspicions when I saw how our culprit came and went without disturbing anyone but his victim. They became stronger when the rats attacked us, and certain when I observed the condition of Olette's mouth."

"I see what you mean."

"And plainly, bards practice a form of magic. You used it to drive the vermin away."

"Well, yes. There's magic in melody, rhythm, and rhyme, and it reveals itself as a bard advances in the craft. But only if you have the knack, and then gradually and perhaps just a little. I can only coax an audience that already likes me into being a little more generous with its appreciation. And occasionally influence animals to do my bidding." She smiled. "It's good for persuading bedbugs to leave you alone."

I snorted. "I've had nights when I could have used that trick."

"You realize, bards aren't the only folk who use magic."

"Of course. But if there were any wizards in town, I'd likely know about it."

If not, it wouldn't be for want of enquiring. It would be a canard to suggest that all such folk are troublemakers. But I had a knack for running afoul of the dastardly ones and had learned to keep an eye out.

"So what now?" Dyllonna asked.

"We go to Pivor's house. I'll find you a bedbug-free place to sleep, and we can consult with him over breakfast."

That turned out to be venison, stork, peaches, and cheat bread among other offerings laid out in a buffet. Pivor cocked his head when Dyllonna and I entered the room. "Isn't that…?" he said.

"Yes," I said, "the lass from the squabble in the square." I introduced them, and the bard bowed in a graceful way that somehow suggested a curtsey even though she was wearing scuffed leather breeches.

Pivor grinned at me. "I had a hunch you wouldn't be able to refrain from poking around."

"You wouldn't have wanted me to," I replied. "Another bard has been attacked. The assailant used magic."

Pivor's air of fashionable nonchalance fell away to reveal the responsible leader he could be when circumstances required. "Tell me."

Dyllonna and I seated ourselves, and then I gave my report.

Afterward, Pivor said, "It's different than the previous victim. Olette didn't have her throat cut."

"Her neck was bleeding. I think she was entranced but at the last instant found the strength to break away, and her attacker feared to pursue her through the crowded house."

Pivor frowned. "Hm."

"I also suspect the actual point of the attack on Edvel was to ruin his mouth and cripple his mind. Killing him simply hid what had befallen him beforehand. When you see a corpse that's manifestly dead of a slashed throat, you assume no further examination is required."

"But why would anyone bother to maim a person in such a way if he was going to kill him immediately afterward?"

"I don't know," I said. "Dyllonna?"

She shook her head. "No idea."

"Here's another problem," Pivor said. "If you're right that a bard did this, which bard? The Plaint is crawling with them."

"Somebody who was present three years ago," I said, "but I doubt that narrows it down very much. So, someone with a motive to harm two gifted singers. Maybe somebody looking to eliminate strong competition in the contests, as Dyllonna suggested. Although that still doesn't explain the maiming."

"It also strikes me as a weak motive," Pivor said. "The children's competitions are important. They determine who gets to study to be a bard and who doesn't. But the adult contests, not as much. The purses are modest, and a singer doesn't need to win to find a berth in a wealthy household. He just has to acquit himself well and strike the fancy of someone with a vacancy."

"There's considerable pride involved," Dyllonna said. "Still, milord, you may have a point."

Essentially, the point was that we understood very little. We glumly mulled that over for a moment.

Then I said, "I have a thought. What if the murders go back more than three years? Milord, would you remember that?"

"I should," Pivor said. "I've been coming here my whole life. Father dragged me along as part of his ongoing campaign to show me that nobles have actual duties and obligations. Let me think…yes! Or possibly yes. Six years ago, a talented singer was killed on the road into town. But that could have been bandits. This country has plenty. Including some of its lords, although you mustn't tell them I said so."

"If the same person," I said, "committed the same crime at the past two festivals, that narrows the field a little more."

"If that's the pattern," Pivor said, "one assault every three years, then at least the worst has already happened." His mouth twisted. "I realize that's a sour way of looking at it."

Dyllonna glowered. "Surely, milord, you aren't saying you intend to do nothing!"

Pivor scowled back. "No, singer, I'm not. My father's lessons took, and I understand I'm responsible for the folk in my dominions, to protect them whenever possible and avenge them when not."

The bard took a breath. "I beg your pardon. I spoke out of turn."

The apology cooled Pivor's temper. "It's all right. I confess, your sense of my priorities may not be entirely off. These deaths matter, but so do other things. So, Selden, I need you to investigate discreetly, without neglecting your other responsibilities, inciting a panic, or giving anyone who matters reason to take offense."

"I understand," I said, "and I know how to begin."

Dyllonna's attack on breakfast demonstrated that she knew how to make the most of a meal that was tasty, plentiful, and free. Then I saddled my mare, commandeered a second horse for her, and we rode out to the bards' school.

It was a collection of one-story structures adjacent to a stand of alders and elms. Students were weeding the gardens and drawing water from the well. Others were singing inside one of the buildings, breaking off when the teacher stopped them, receiving his criticism, and then attempting the same passage again.

Dyllonna and I repaired to the largest building. There I informed yet another pupil, this one playing doorman, that we needed to speak to the masters on a matter of urgency. On our first try, we got four of them, who met us in a room containing several large harps and a miscellany of other instruments.

"I'd hoped to consult with all seven of you," I said.

A woman with hair dyed a bright and unnatural shade of gold smiled as if I'd said something foolish. "Master…Selden, was it?…you've come at the least convenient time imaginable. We have to judge the competitions while also rehearsing the performances we'll give as the finale to the festival. You're lucky we four have even a little time to spare."

I stared her in the eye. "I respect you masters, but as long as you care to dwell in this place, Pivor is your lord, and as his representative, I'll have some respect in return. Especially since a bard is murdering other bards utilizing the secrets of your craft"—their eyes widened—"and I need your help to identify him. Now, please send for the others."

She dispatched the doorman, and they turned up one by one, including he who appeared to be the oldest of them all, wrinkled, white-bearded, and walking with the aid of a silver-handled cane. He still seemed fairly spry, though, with clear gray eyes that were shrewd and none too friendly.

"I'm Lendach," he said, "the leader of this circle. What is this nonsense?"

I told him, and at the end, I said, "I need to understand the purpose of this blighting magic and who knows how to use it."

The other masters looked to Lendach. Plainly, they believed he'd be the one to know if anyone did. But he shook his head and said, "There is no such song."

"Could you take a moment to think about it?" I replied. "Something unnatural befell Olette."

"Then look for a sorcerer or vampire. No bard could do such a thing."

"Did Olette have a rival who might have wished to do it if he could?"

"No."

We back-and-forthed a while longer, with Lendach providing the answers and his fellows endorsing them with their silence. Finally, Dyllonna and I took our leave.

Back out in the sunlight, I said, "Considering that Olette is one of your own, I find their level of sympathy unimpressive. They must have been a delight to study under."

Dyllonna smiled crookedly. "Especially if you were one of the unimpressive pupils. Seriously, they aren't all so bad. But once Lendach made it clear that in his judgment, we were bothering them with foolishness…"

"Yes, Lendach, who was ever so busy preparing for his concert. What would happen if he embarrassed himself with a bad one?"

"It would be a disgrace, obviously."

"What if the performance was bad enough to cast doubt on his fitness to be a master bard?"

"I suppose the other members of the inner circle might insist that he step down. But why are you asking? Lendach will do well. He may be old, but as you just heard for yourself, his voice is still melodious and his mind is still sharp."

"Yes," I said, "aren't they, though?"

I looked around and spied a lanky fellow of about my own age in a broad-brimmed straw hat. He was slouching in the shade of an alder watching the student gardeners. There had to be a couple such permanent workers here to make sure the young singers actually got their chores done.

I headed over to him with Dyllonna trailing after me. I gave him a smile and said, "It's a nice morning."

He grunted.

"Are you going to the festival later on?"

He shrugged.

"Perhaps you'd enjoy it more with some extra silver in your purse."

The suggestion didn't make him friendlier, exactly, but at least it moved him to speech. "What do you want?"

"A little information about the masters."

He frowned. "They wouldn't want me gossiping."

"Then we'll keep it among the three of us." I opened my belt pouch and scooped out several coins. "Do you want these or not?"

"Ask."

"Think back six or seven years. Was there a period when Lendach's health seemed to be failing? If so, did it affect his music or his thinking?"

My informant nodded. "He had a fit and wasn't himself for a while after. But then he got better. How'd you know?"

I gave him the silver. "Thanks. Enjoy the festival."

As Dyllonna and I walked back to the horses, she said, "I see what your idea is. But it's pure speculation."

"Remember that the person who attacked Olette couldn't simply outdistance us even though he had a head start. He limped. At the time, I thought that perhaps he hurt himself jumping out the casement, but it was only a short hop to the ground. Perhaps he was actually limping like an old man who carries a cane."

"Hm."

"Consider too that when discussing Olette's affliction, Lendach used the specific term 'vampire.' Not ghost or demon, 'vampire.' What if that was a slip?"

"You mean, what if, after his seizure, he couldn't bear the prospect of being less than he was and forced from his office? So he used evil magic to steal the physical and mental qualities that make a bard to restore his own powers? And needs to repeat the process at intervals?"

I nodded. "He'd likely be found out if he preyed on people here at the school. But he might well go uncaught at big, chaotic gatherings of all the bards and hundreds of other folk from across the southlands."

Dyllonna shook her head. "You make the notion sound halfway plausible, but it still just seems like guesswork. I don't want you to make a fool of yourself with a false accusation. Arrogant pig though he is, I'll be a long time living down my denunciations of Rogros."

I patted my mare's neck, then untied her reins from the hitching post. "Trust me, I have no intention of accusing the chief of the bards without proof. That's why I'm coming back after dark, to look for it. Will you help? You're the one who knows her way around."

Dyllonna pulled a wry face. "The order could cast me out if this goes amiss. But yes, of course."

I spent the remaining daylight hours keeping order in town and, without being obvious about it, making sure my men-at-arms were prepared to operate without me later on. Dyllonna and I rode back to the college after dark.

We left the horses tied at the back of the grove and skulked up through the trees. On first inspection, the school looked as deserted as I'd hoped. Still, it was likely someone was about, so we kept sneaking as Dyllonna led me to the cottage that was Lendach's residence.

To my surprise, given the bucolic setting, the door had a citified lock, and the master bard had engaged it. "I keep meaning to learn to pick these," I whispered, lifting my foot for a kick.

"Let me," Dyllonna replied. She knelt down, extracted a set of picks and torsion tools from inside her jerkin, and set to work. The lock clicked, and the door swung ajar.

"Nicely done. Is that part of the curriculum here?"

"It should be. Folk aren't always generous out on the road." She stowed away her burglar's kit and stood up. "Let's get inside."

We left the door cracked, opened the shutters just a little, and that provided just enough light to search by. Dyllonna examined a shelf of books and scrolls, carrying them to the window when that proved necessary to make out the writing. Reasoning that if there was evidence of dark magic to be found, Lendach might not have left it sitting out in the open, I looked for a hiding place.

Eventually I rapped, heard a hollow sound, and fumbled open the hidden panel in the back of a wardrobe. Then I flinched as the sheaf of parchment inside the hitherto concealed cubby gave off a pulse of malignancy. If you've ever come into contact with accursed artifacts or the like, perhaps you know the sensation.

I swallowed and, when I was sure I wasn't going to puke, said, "Look at these if you can stomach it."

Dyllonna picked them up, then sucked in her breath as if they'd given her fingers a sting. After that, though, she was able to handle them without discomfort. She went the window and started to riffle through them.

Eventually she said, "I don't understand all of this. It's based on lore I was never taught and wouldn't care to be. But it's a collection of songs for hurting people, calling on devils, and doing other terrible things."

"That's a start. But a master bard could argue that it's proper for him to possess such papers as long as he doesn't actually cast the spells. We need—"

"I know." She skimmed three more pages, then came upon one that warranted a more careful reading. "This is it! The song for stealing another bard's abilities!"

"The song Lendach claimed didn't exist."

"There are even notes in a different hand and in darker, newer ink at the bottom of the parchment!"

"We should have no difficulty obtaining other samples of Lendach's handwriting to compare that writing to. Which clinches it. Evdel's killer is going to the gallows."

Dyllonna swallowed. "I knew I was going to try. But I didn't know if I could really…I mean…" She started crying.

I squeezed her shoulder. "This is no time for tears. This is the moment for joyous retribution."

"You're right." She snuffled and swiped at her nose and eyes. "If we hurry, we can denounce him in front of the whole town!"

That sounded satisfying to me as well, and I was eager to have at it as we hurried back to the horses and mounted up. Then I started to hurt.

My rat bites had been itching and smarting off and on all day, and at first I imagined the discomfort was simply more of the same. But it flowered in spots where the rodents' teeth hadn't pierced me, and as Dyllonna and I reached the road back into the Plaint, it erupted into genuine torment. I let out a strangled cry.

Dyllonna turned in the saddle to look at me. "Oh, no," she breathed.

"What's wrong with me?" I asked.

"Boils."

I raised a trembling hand and touched one of the newly risen bumps on my face. That was a mistake. The slightest pressure made it throb even worse.

"It's said," Dyllonna told me, "that in olden times, an accomplished bard could compose a satire against a lord or official, and the performance would raise boils on the target's face. Lendach must have taken to the stage tonight to ridicule you."

Because the gardener I'd questioned had tattled. Or maybe the things I'd said to Lendach himself had sufficed to make him worry I was sniffing too close to the truth.

"Well, if this is his best defense," I gritted, "he's finished. It takes more than a little pain to silence me."

"You don't understand. The real purpose of a satire was to make the victim an object of general dislike and contempt. Lendach's trying to fix it so no one will heed you." She hesitated. "Perhaps I should accuse him."

I shook my head, and the boils on my neck gave me pangs. "You said it yourself. You undermined your credibility by falsely accusing Rogros, and Lendach's an important man. If you denounce him, he'll brazen it out, the evidence notwithstanding. It has to be me, Pivor's deputy and friend."

She looked dubious, but she gave me a nod. We urged our mounts onward.

Haste too was arguably a mistake given the boils on my rump and inner thighs. But I thought a swift ride preferable to a more protracted, gentler one, especially as I planned to force Lendach to lift the curse he'd cast on me at the end of it.

The punishment wrung gasps, grunts, and the occasional profanity out of me, though, and after one such exclamation, Dyllonna sneered and said, "It's your own fault. If you were any good at your profession, you would have found the truth sooner, before Lendach had a chance to do this to you."

My pains urged me to respond with the same sort of spite, but then I realized what was actually happening. "Steady," I said. "The spell is corrupting your opinion of me."

She stiffened. "I…I think it was! I'm sorry!"

"It wasn't your fault. But keep your head straight."

We reached the edge of town not long after.

No doubt the greatest concentration of folk was in the square where the singers were competing, their voices intermittently audible even at a distance. But not everyone could squeeze in, and the streets radiating out from it were crowded, too, with revelers enjoying the antics of dancing dogs, jugglers, and puppeteers. Dyllonna and I had to slow our horses to a walk.

That gave people a chance to notice who was trying to ride through their midst. First, they glared, and then they catcalled.

"Coward!"

"Liar!"

"Pervert!"

Next, a flung rock hit a boil on my cheek. I jerked and cried out, and a sound went up from the mob that was half laugh and half roar. Certain more missiles would follow, I crouched down as best I could in the saddle and started to kick the mare into a faster gait. I still didn't want to ride over anyone, but I wasn't eager to endure a stoning, either.

Then a spearman with Pivor's coat of arms embroidered on his livery pushed his way through the crowd. Specifically, it was stolid, gap-toothed Beck, one of the soldiers my patron had placed under my direction.

"I need your help!" I said.

He spat. "After abandoning us to do all the work by ourselves? Where have you been?"

"Attending to Lord Pivor's business! I order you—"

Beck plunged his spear into my horse's neck.

The mare threw her head back, then fell. I kicked free of the stirrups and made an awkward leap.

That kept me from ending up pinned beneath the animal's convulsing body. But by the time I found my balance, Beck was coming at me. He'd left the spear in the mare's neck and drawn his sword.

I sprang back, and his first cut missed. I snatched out my blade, parried his second attack, started to riposte with a stroke that could have crippled his hand forever after, and then remembered he wasn't to blame for his malice. I stopped the slash short of the target.

He hacked at my kidney. I parried, then, maintaining pressure on his sword, immobilizing it, shifted in close. I smashed my pommel into his jaw, and he reeled backward and fell.

Good. But when I looked around, other folk were converging on me with their knives or whatever makeshift weapon had been ready to hand. Turning, I balked the nearest with feints, a tactic that wouldn't hold them back for long.

Then Dyllonna forced her way toward me. Her staff rose and fell, cracking skulls. It was a clumsy weapon to use one-handed or astride a horse for that matter, but aggression and the animal's bulk opened a path through my assailants.

I scrambled up behind Dyllonna and slashed someone's face. He would have caught hold of her belt and dragged her from the saddle if I hadn't.

The splash of blood and his squeal gave the other attackers pause, and Dyllonna managed to turn her horse and gallop back the way we'd come. Angry shouts and a shower of stones pursued up, but we made it back out of town.

When we felt safe, we dismounted, and Dyllonna crooned praise and reassurance to her trembling mount. By touch, I examined my cheek and found a mess of blood and pus. The first stone had burst the boil, which, to my disgust, didn't make the spot hurt any less.

At least the pain attendant upon my disfigurement hadn't hindered me during the fight. My focus on the exigencies of the moment blocked it out. That was something.

Still, I felt ill used, and my tone was petulant as I observed, "You said the satire would incline people to disrespect me. You didn't warn me it would turn them into mad dogs."

"That's not how it worked in the old accounts. Lendach must have found an especially poisonous version of the song."

"Well, how long is the effect supposed to last?"

Her mouth tightened. "Until the bard dissolves it, or something breaks his power."

"Plainly, we need to try for the latter. That means you need to sing a song to dilute its influence."

She blinked. "I told you, my music is only mediocre."

"A mediocrity that makes rats docile and crowds friendly. You know the necessary tricks."

"Do you want to gamble your life that I know them well enough to overcome the magic of the greatest bard in the southlands?"

"Lendach already performed his satire. The mob will be hearing your song as you sing it. Perhaps that will give you an edge. In any case, I can't stay as I am, and you can't let Edvel's murder go unavenged."

She took a deep breath. "Wait, and be quiet. It will take some time to put the song together."

She prowled around in the moonlight humming bits of melody and muttering under her breath. I pondered the advisability of lancing boils with a dagger point and decided not to make the experiment.

Eventually she turned to face me. "Just so you know," she said, "I don't really see you as the paragon the verses describe."

I chuckled. "I'll try not to take it to heart." I waved my hand toward the horse. "Shall we?"

She frowned. "I can ride, but I'm no expert. I've certainly never practiced singing while bouncing and swaying on horseback. If you want my song to be as potent as it can be…"

She didn't have to spell out the tradeoff. If her magic failed to calm the throng, accomplishing a second retreat would be more problematic on foot.

"We'll leave the poor animal to graze in peace," I said. "He's been through enough for one evening."

She started singing when we were twenty paces from the edge of town. Her vibrant alto voice seemed sweet and rich to my admittedly untutored ear. As promised, the song of Selden was a catalogue of stainless virtues and impossible heroisms that occasionally drew inspiration from my more notorious real-life exploits, like slaying the fire spirit and the undead magus Yshan Keenspur.

When people recognized me, their faces twisted. Fortunately, Dyllonna's song then touched them, and they faltered, some looking shocked at themselves, like they'd just awakened from a dream of doing something vile, others, perplexed and uncertain.

I still wanted to stride quickly but recognized that my companion couldn't do that and sing to best effect, either. She had to glide along in what amounted to a stately dance, turning from side to side to further charm the crowd with her gaze and her smile, and I had to hold myself to the same pace.

It wore my nerves to rags. Still, her tactics worked. We made it to the square without anyone else attacking us, although a number of scowling folk trailed along behind us as though the itch was still present.

Pivor, the mayor, and the high bards were all seated on an elevated platform for dignitaries. Lendach goggled at me, no doubt flummoxed that I'd made it here alive.

When the youth singing on the main stage realized I'd distracted everyone from his performance, he fell silent. Meanwhile, Dyllonna kept crooning her counterspell. But softly now, so I could make myself heard above the melody.

"Lendach," I called, "by the authority vested in me by Lord Pivor, I arrest you for murder!"

The master bard forced a laugh. "That's absurd! And in any case, Pivor now understands your incompetence and dishonesty, and he's stripped you of your position! Isn't that right, my lord?"

The nobleman looked back and forth between Lendach and me uncertainly. To some degree, he was still under the old man's sway. But, nudged by Dyllonna's power, he now recalled our friendship and all I'd done for his family and our city.

"I can prove what I say!" I held up the sheaf of parchments. "Songs of dark magic with notes appended in your hand! I ask the other high bards to inspect them!"

Lendach rose from his chair. "You insult me, and in so doing, you insult our sacred fellowship and its traditions. Rest assured, I will defend our honor."

With that, he started singing, if that was the proper word for it. It was a wail like a wolf pack howling together. He also stalked toward the edge of the platform, each pace surer and heavier than the last, and as he came toward me, he changed.

His upper body swelled, putting on muscle, until his robe ripped at the seams. His torso hitched forward, too, transforming him into something akin to a hunchback. His fingernails extended into jagged claws, his arms stretched longer than his legs, and the lower part of his face bulged into a slavering muzzle full of fangs. His ears sprouted points, the gray eyes turned yellow, and his body hair thickened into a coat of snow-white fur.

In short, he became a bestial horror that unquestionably looked capable of slaughtering a boil-ridden human swordsman. I assumed he meant to kill Dyllonna, too, and reduce the incriminating parchments to shredded, blood-soaked illegibility.

As I stuffed them in my shirt, I said, "You didn't warn me he could do this, either."

Dyllonna shook her head to say she hadn't known, hefted her staff, and started to move up beside me.

"No!" I snapped. "Stay back and concentrate on your singing!" If she hit a false note or missed a beat, the crowd might rush in to help Lendach rip me apart.

His transformation complete, the high bard sprang off the platform. I snatched my dagger from its sheath and threw it. A target can't dodge when he's in midair.

Unfortunately, he can parry. With more speed than I'd hoped to see, Lendach slapped the blade in midflight and sent it tumbling away.

As soon as his feet touched the ground, he came at me. I retreated before him until I had the broadsword out. He struck at the blade with a backhand swipe of his fist.

The blow nearly bashed the hilt from my grip. It did knock the weapon out of line, and he lunged and raked with his other hand. I jumped back just in time to keep his claws from ripping away my eyes.

Then we circled. The sword gave me an advantage in reach, but given his freakishly long arms, only barely, and his speed, strength, and unnatural hardiness offset it. He was willing to suffer cuts to his hands and forearms for the chance to beat my weapon to the side again, or better yet, disarm me, and I could see why. Though bloody, the wounds to his extremities weren't slowing him down.

I needed to strike him in the vitals. I was still pondering how when he grabbed my blade.

Without an armored gauntlet, no merely human combatant would do that for fear of losing fingers. But Lendach jerked me toward him and opened his jaws.

I couldn't use the sword, nor, without letting go of it, could I withstand the pull. As the beast-man's head shot forward to bite into mine, I stabbed my stiffened fingers into a yellow eye.

The shock of that froze him, and I floundered clear, dragging the sword free in the process. But it took me an instant to come back on guard, and that gave him time to do the same.

Panting, sweat burning in my eyes, I cut to the knee. Lendach smashed his fist down on my weapon, and I dropped it.

Goggling in what I hoped looked like panic, I recoiled. Lendach threw himself at me. Why not? I was defenseless.

I sidestepped, he plunged past me, and the momentum of that top-heavy, hunched-over frame made it difficult to stop. I had the sword back in my hand by the time he started to turn around.

My first cut sheared into his neck, and my second cut his spine. He pitched to the ground, and the third one split his skull.

Pivor gawked down at me. "Bright Angels! Did you drop the sword on purpose?" He was speaking to me as he would to a friend.

I grinned. "I had a hunch that if I didn't finish the fight quickly, it would end up going his way. So I tried a trick to get behind him." I pulled the parchments back out of my shirt. "You really should examine these."

With Lendach's curse broken, the other high bards affirmed that the papers proved his guilt. The only unsatisfactory thing about the end of the affair was that while everyone stopped despising me, the boils didn't instantly disappear. I had to return to the physician to have them lanced and ended up more covered in ointment and plasters than before.

The effect was more comical than seductive. Still, when I dined with Dyllonna the following night, I made bold to say, "I see why Edvel chose your company whenever your paths crossed. I'd be inclined to do the same."

"I'm afraid," she replied, her lips greasy and a chicken wing in her hand, "that will seldom happen. Lord Bluegarden offered me a place in his household. Apparently my performance in the square impressed him, and he too appreciates a good joke as much as a good tune."

I sighed. "He's lucky to have you."

She smiled. "But you and I are together now. Let's see where the night takes us."